THE SALOON'S BACK DOOR
CRASHED OPEN . . .

Gabe saw the gleam of a pistol in the man's hand, so he fired, not trying to hit the man himself, but rather sending the bullet into the doorframe, where it sprayed splinters into the gunman's face.

"He's still in the alley," a voice shouted from inside the barroom. "Let's get around to the sides, pin him down before he gets away."

That was a thought that had already occurred to Gabe, both getting away, plus the danger of finding himself trapped from either end. He began to run down the alley in the direction of the stables.

There were shouts from behind him. "There he goes!" one man yelled. Guns crashed. Bullets whacked into nearby walls, and plowed up dirt ahead of Gabe.

He had almost reached the mouth of the alley when he saw dark figures ahead. "That's him!" someone shouted . . .

Books in the LONG RIDER *series from Charter*

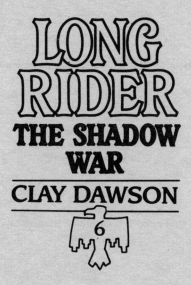

LONG RIDER

THE SHADOW WAR

CLAY DAWSON

6

CHARTER BOOKS, NEW YORK

THE SHADOW WAR

A Charter Book/published by arrangement with
the author

PRINTING HISTORY
Charter edition/September 1989

ISBN: 1-55773-252-3

PRINTED IN THE UNITED STATES OF AMERICA

10 9 8 7 6 5 4 3 2 1

CHAPTER ONE

He appeared out of the darkness quite suddenly, soundlessly. One moment he was not there, the next moment he was, seated, motionless, on a tall horse at the edge of the woods that bordered the town.

Two drunks had just left the local saloon. One of them had seen the stranger materialize out of the woods. "Jesus, Hank, looka that," he said, tugging at his partner's sleeve, while he pointed toward the stranger.

Hank looked. "Whassa matter?" he muttered. "Jus' a man on a horse."

However, he too was caught by the motionlessness of the rider, who was apparently studying the town's single, dusty main street. "Injun?" Hank asked cautiously. Indians were still feared in this area, the land having recently been theirs.

The horseman began to move, guiding his mount away from the woods and out into the street, toward the drunks. "God yes . . . Injun," Hank muttered.

As the rider drew closer, Hank's companion shook his head. "Uh-uh. White man. See? He's wearin' a hat."

"I seen Injuns wear hats."

"But look at his hair. That ain't no Injun hair, even if it's long like an Injun's."

The man's hair was indeed long. But now that he was closer, Hank could see, even in the dim evening light, that the rider's hair was quite light in color, almost blond. Nor were his clothes the kind of clothes an Indian might choose. The light-colored linen duster that he wore was not fastened in front, and beneath the duster his clothes were white man's clothes. As he passed by, Hank muttered once more, "Well . . . he rides just like a goddamned Injun."

The rider had, of course, noticed the two drunks, and for a moment had felt uneasy about turning his back on them as he passed by. But a quick assessment, made without turning his head toward them, convinced him that they were what they seemed to be . . . harmless drunks.

Still, he felt slightly uneasy. He always felt uneasy in the white man's towns, for, unlike Hank and his bottle companion, the rider did not think of himself as a white man.

Then why am I here? he silently asked himself. For supplies, of course. But as he asked himself the question again, he had to admit that he was also here out of curiosity, to satisfy that itch inside himself that always made him want to see, to know, to taste things. And he had been wondering for several days what it would be like in this particular white man's town, a town that had sprung up overnight on this sacred ground that had so recently been taken from The People.

He was about to pass the saloon from which the two drunks had come, when he suddenly halted his horse. He did not like saloons, he did not like the feel of them, but he also knew that in white towns, a saloon was sometimes useful for getting the feel of the place.

So he pulled his horse up to the hitching rack in front of the saloon, dismounted, and tied the horse's reins to the rack. He hesitated for a moment before leaving his mount, then, having reached a decision, he drew his two rifles from their saddle scabbards. Carrying a rifle in each hand, he pushed in through the saloon's swinging doors.

There were only about a dozen men inside. It had been a dull night so far, so most of the saloon's inmates turned to see who was coming in through the doors, and as soon as they saw, some decided that it might not turn out to be such a dull night after all.

The stranger was tall, about six foot two, and strongly built. His long linen duster, somewhat stained from trail wear, hung nearly to his ankles. It had swung open far enough so that his clothing was visible underneath: a dark shirt, dark trousers, a large dark neckerchief hanging down onto his chest, and, instead of boots, a pair of soft Indian moccasins. A gunbelt rode fairly high around his waist, although the folds of the duster hid any pistols he might be wearing.

The man stood in the doorway for a moment, a rifle in each hand, and a few of the men standing closer to the door, edged back. It was not only the rifles, it was the man himself, the way he stood, motionless, surveying the room. He wore a large, dark slouch hat, the brim low enough so that it was difficult to see his eyes. His face was very dark, either sun-darkened or naturally dark; in the poor lighting it was difficult to tell. Once again men thought of Indians, which confused them, as it had the two drunks outside, because of the long sandy-colored hair that escaped from under the drooping brim of the hat, and the color of his eyes, which, when he turned to look toward the bar, proved to be very light in color.

Having appraised the situation, and having decided that it was tolerable, the stranger moved over to a table, one set against the front wall, not far from the door. He propped both rifles against the wall, then walked over to the bar, and as he walked, the linen duster moved far enough away from his body so that it was possible to see the pistol he wore, on his right hip, butt forward, cavalry style, except that he was not using a cavalry holster with its protective flap. The stranger's holster was cut low, with part of the trigger guard and cylinder showing. A fighting man's rig.

The bartender moved over toward the stranger. He caught a glimpse of those light gray eyes half-hidden by the brim of the hat. "What'll it be, stranger?" the bartender asked.

"Sarsaparilla. A big glass."

"What?" the bartender asked, surprised.

"If you haven't got sarsaparilla, root beer will do."

The words were said in a flat, controlled voice. The bartender wished he could see those eyes more clearly. "We got sarsaparilla," he muttered.

He went to fill a glass. Half-smothered laughter sounded from further back in the room, but the stranger ignored it, continuing to stand easily at the bar. When the bartender had brought him his glass of sarsaparilla, he turned and went back to his table, where he sat down, his back to the heavy log wall, facing the rest of the room, with the front door about ten feet to his left.

Before he drank, he took off his hat and laid it on the table. His hair now hung free, cascading back over his shoulders. He shook his head, seeming to like the feel of not wearing his hat. Then he took a sip of his sarsaparilla.

There was more half-smothered laughter from the rear of the room. A party of half a dozen cowhands were clustered around two tables. They had been drinking for a couple of hours, and were fairly well drunk, feeling wild and hairy. There was a little muttering among them, and then one stood up and headed toward the stranger. Two more got up and followed him.

The cowboy moved next to the stranger's table. "You a teetotal, mister?" the cowboy asked in a harsh Texas twang.

The stranger said nothing, kept looking straight down at the table top. The cowboy was not about to go away. "You some kinda bible-thumper," he continued, "sayin' the Good Book don't hold for a man wettin' his whistle with a little pop-skull now and then?"

The stranger finally replied, but continued to look down toward the table. "I don't care to drink. I've seen drinking turn good men into bad men. Too many times."

Encouraged by the man's failure to meet his gaze, the cowboy began to feel bolder. "You suggestin' I'm no good, mister? 'Cause I sure as hell like to drink."

There was a good deal of guffawing from the cowboy's companions, but when the stranger answered, his voice was still calm, emotionless. "I have not known you long enough to know if you are a good man or a bad man."

Now the cowhand was beginning to grow irritated. "What the hell kinda answer is that, mister? Say, what's your name, anyhow?"

The stranger took a sip of his sarsaparilla. "Some men call me Gabe."

The cowhand grinned. "Tell you what, Gabe. I'm gonna buy you a whiskey. I hope to hell you'll let me buy you a whiskey."

"If that's what you want."

The cowboy strode over to the bar. The bartender had heard and was already pouring the drink. The cowboy took it back to the stranger's table. "Here ya go, Gabe," he said genially.

The stranger nodded as the glass was placed on the table in front of him, but he still did not look up. The cowboy waited expectantly as Gabe's hand reached out. The cowboy noticed that the stranger's right index finger was bent out sharply near the first joint, and for some reason that bothered him a little. But what bothered him even more was when he saw that it was the glass of sarsaparilla that the stranger was picking up. He was taking a sip of the sarsaparilla when the cowboy exploded. "What the hell's the matter with you, stranger? You too damned good to drink my whiskey?"

The stranger quietly took another sip of sarsaparilla. The cowboy, feeling bold with two friends close behind him and three more back at his table, leaned his weight on the stranger's table. "You'll drink with me, you son of a bitch, or I'll . . . ."

The cowboy's voice faded away, because the stranger had finally looked up, meeting his gaze, and the cowboy found himself looking into as cold a pair of eyes as he'd ever seen.

Light gray eyes, so light that they seemed almost colorless. Eyes which appeared to have no emotion at all in them. Eyes that trapped his own with their remorseless power. "Are you so ready to die?" the stranger asked in that same quiet voice.

The cowboy did not answer, but instead backed slowly away from the stranger's table. The stranger's eyes followed him, and the cowhand backpedalled another half-dozen steps, until he ran into another table. The stranger took a final sip of his sarsaparilla, then stood up, retrieved his rifles, and headed for the door. It was only when he had disappeared into the darkness outside that the cowboy realized he was not breathing. He quickly took in a long shuddering gasp of air.

The other three cowhands now came up front from their table. "What the hell happened, Joe?" one of them asked scornfully. "Did you let that long-haired sarsaparilla-drinkin' sissy buffalo you?"

Joe shook his head and swallowed. "There just wasn't nothin' in his eyes," he murmured. "None of the things that are supposed to be in a man's eyes. There was nothin' there at all."

"Shit," the newcomer sneered. "You let . . . ."

"Shut up, Hank," another man said, one of the ones who'd accompanied Joe to the stranger's table. "You wasn't there. If you was . . . hell . . . it reminded me of somethin' I saw about two years back."

"What was that?" Joe asked.

"It was an Injun. A Hunkpapa Sioux. I saw him lookin' at a white man just the way that teetotal looked at you."

"And . . . ?" Joe prompted.

The man shuddered. "Then the Injun pulled out a knife, pulled it as fast as you can blink an eye . . . and gutted that white man right in front of a whole room full o' people."

CHAPTER TWO

Once back out in the night, Gabe returned his rifles to their saddle scabbards, then mounted his horse and continued on down the street. Although his face retained the same unemotional expression as it had inside the bar, he was angry . . . mostly with himself. He had meant to avoid trouble, had done his best to be polite to the men inside the bar, even to the drunken cowhands.

Unfortunately, he had used the politeness he'd been brought up to believe was right, and not the white man's politeness. All through the encounter with the cowhand, he had politely kept his eyes lowered, fastened on the table top, forgetting that to a white man, looking another man straight in the eye was not the insulting challenge he had grown up believing it to be.

And he had been ready to kill that cowboy. He had been warned that killing was a big thing to a white man, although they killed often enough. But they had different ways of justifying it. To him, in the bar, it had been man to man, the cowhand challenging him, himself ready to take up the challenge.

It had never occurred to him to excuse the cowhand simply

because he was drunk. That would have been the greatest possible insult, as if the cowhand was not a man, not capable of choosing his own path, as men did. Alcohol was no excuse, it was a path in itself, one a man was free to take, or not take. No, a man was a man, and once he chose a path, he must be allowed to follow it to its end, to accept the responsibility for his own actions. Even if the final result was that man's own death.

But the cowhand had backed down, he had turned out to be a coward, the only brave thing about him being his empty words. Gabe had almost killed him because of his cowardice alone. The kindest thing one could do for a coward was to kill him, before his cowardice infected others.

Or so Gabe had been taught originally, before he began to move among the whites, before he had been tutored in the white man's way. Tonight, he had temporarily forgotten those ways. Perhaps it was fatigue. He was tired from the trail, from the long ride. It would be a good idea to sleep, so that he would awaken in the morning with his mind and body fresh. And perhaps not make any more mistakes.

He considered riding on out of town and making camp along the trail. But there were too many people here now, and his camp might be discovered and attract attention. Some of The People might even find him, and considering him just another white man, attack him.

He saw the words, Rooms For Rent painted on a board that hung from the front porch of a house. It would be less noticeable if he stayed in town tonight, like any other white man, although he hated the thought of a house, its confining walls, the musty smells, the rigidity of it, the distance it would take him from his mother, the Earth.

However, he tied his horse to the hitching rack in front of the house, walked up the steps, and knocked on the door. The door opened a crack, giving him a view of part of a woman's face. "Yes?" the woman asked suspiciously. It occurred to Gabe that many of the people in this town seemed to be afraid of one another.

"I would like a room for the night," he said politely, looking the woman straight in the eye.

For a moment or two she said nothing, but studied him carefully, noting that, although he was dusty and stained from the trail, there was a general cleanliness and neatness about him, and she had been brought up believing that cleanliness is next to Godliness. "You one of those buffalo hunters?" she asked, eyeing his long hair.

"No ma'am . . . just a weary traveler."

"Your name? I don't talk to gentlemen without names."

"Conrad, ma'am. Gabe Conrad."

"Well, Mr. Conrad, I don't normally rent rooms for just one night, but, seein' as you're so tired . . . ."

"Thank you, ma'am."

She opened the door wider. "I'm Mrs. Lukens. If you'd like to see the room first . . . ."

He could see now that the woman was perhaps in her fifties, although this land aged women fast. "Mrs. Lukens, if it's got a bed, I'm sure it'll be all right. Maybe even if it hasn't got a bed. But first . . . my horse . . . ."

"Sure 'nough. There's a stable 'round back. You'll have to see to the horse yourself. Cain't afford no hired help here since my husband passed on. When you got him put up, jus' knock on the back door."

Gabe nodded, then led his horse around to the back of the house. He spent the next ten minutes unsaddling the animal, and replacing the bit and bridle with a flexible hackamore, which he himself had woven out of horsehair. If he needed his mount fast, there'd be a headstall to control the animal, but the horse would be more comfortable, better able to feed itself, than if he'd left the bit and bridle in place.

Lugging his bedroll, saddlebags, and rifles, he made his way to the back door, which opened before he had a chance to knock, which was fortunate for Gabe considering how he was loaded down. The woman held the door open and he went by her into a narrow hallway, facing a flight of stairs. "Head of the stairs, Mr. Conrad. First door on the right."

A little warmth had come into her voice, now that she knew this stranger for a quiet, polite customer rather than possible trouble. He nodded, headed in the direction she'd indicated, and found himself in a simple room, with a narrow bed, a small rug on the floor next to the bed, a wash basin, and a tiny closet. He placed his gear on the floor, and by the time he'd opened his saddle bags, the woman had returned with a pitcher of water, which she put down next to the basin. "There's a wash house out back, if you need it," she informed him, although he got the impression she considered it a little late in the evening for lengthy ablutions.

"No thanks, Mrs. Lukens. This is enough," he said quietly. She nodded, then withdrew, closing the door after her.

After listening to the woman's footsteps fade away down the stairs, Gabe took off his linen duster, revealing not only the pistol holstered on his right hip, but a twin to the first pistol, housed in a holster that fitted underneath his right arm. A knife sheath had been sewn alongside the shoulder holster, with the handle of the knife pointing downward within easy reach. He took off the gunbelt and shoulder holster, then laid the pistols and the knife on the floor next to the bed, alongside his rifles.

After propping the room's only chair underneath the doorknob, Gabe pulled off his moccasins, trousers, and shirt, then poured a little water from the pitcher into the basin and washed his hands, face, and torso, sponging away the sweat and grit he'd picked up on the trail. Finally, he lay down on the bed and pulled the single thin woolen blanket over his body.

But, tired as he was, he found it difficult to fall asleep. The bed, made of cheap springs stretched over a metal framework, sagged. And the coarse wool of the blanket irritated his skin. His mind wandered for a moment, and he remembered the beautiful buffalo robes his mother had fashioned for him, all those years ago. He remembered the buttery softness of the interior skin, the warmth of the fur, the comforting odor of himself and his mother that permeated the robe.

He remembered his firm bed, resting on the clean, swept ground inside the lodge. He remembered the sound of his sleeping mother's soft breathing nearby. He also remembered the sense of belonging, the security of knowing that The People were all about him, asleep in their lodges.

He got up, put the thin cotton mattress on the floor and lay down again. He was more comfortable now, at least in body. But what a lonely place this was, despite the great number of people in the town, so many horribly separated individuals, all shut up in small wooden boxes, each one so isolated. That, he would never grow used to.

CHAPTER THREE

Gabe awoke a little before dawn. He was tempted to get up immediately to begin his day, but he knew that the town would not begin its own day for a while yet, and he needed the town. So he lay on the mattress for a while, until, when the first light was showing in the east, he got up, returned the mattress to the bed frame, washed again at the hand basin, dressed, packed up his gear and weapons, and started down the stairs.

Mrs. Lukens also proved to be an early riser. She met him when he was only halfway down the stairs. Gabe saw a moment's suspicion on her face, but he instantly allayed it by saying, "I left the fifty cents for the room on the bed."

Mrs. Lukens beamed, the first full smile he'd seen from her so far. "Come on into the kitchen, then. You get breakfast, too, for that fifty cents."

Gabe was about to decline, then decided that a good breakfast would not be a bad thing at all. He dumped his gear, including the rifles, in the hallway, then went out to the stable to ready his mount while Mrs. Lukens busied herself in the kitchen. After saddling and bridling his horse, he went back into the house, stepping into an aroma of frying meat and baking bread, which made the kitchen very easy to find.

He ate at a massive old table set in a corner of the big kitchen. The table was obviously quite a bit older than the house itself, which, like most of the local buildings was fairly new, even if it did show signs of premature weathering. In this part of the territory, not too much care, not too much permanence, went into the average structure. It was boom or bust country, and no one knew when the mad movement of settlers, gamblers, miners, or cattlemen might sweep on by, leaving ghost towns behind.

"Am I your only guest?" Gabe asked Mrs. Lukens, as she brought a big plate of dripping bacon over to the table.

" 'Fraid so, Mr. Conrad. They built a real honest to goodness hotel over to the other side o' the church. Gets most of the transient trade, and right now I'm in between boarders."

"That certainly turned out lucky for me," Gabe replied, cutting into an egg that had been fried in bacon drippings, smearing the yolk over his bacon. "I haven't had a breakfast like this for a long time."

Mrs. Lukens flushed with pleasure. "Hard enough around here for a widow woman. Without a man . . . ."

She looked wistfully in Gabe's direction, then sensibly turned back to the oven, from which she was pulling another batch of fresh-baked biscuits. Yet she could not help herself from thinking admiring thoughts about this stranger, this rather odd Mr. Conrad, with his tall strong frame and his outlandishly long hair. His face, and those parts of his body that showed, were very dark, as if the sun had been baking him for years, as if he spent every possible waking moment out of doors. She tried to remember the last time she'd had much to do with a man's body, particularly one as fine-looking as Mr. Conrad's, and when she realized what she was thinking, she went red with shame and confusion.

Which was not helped when Gabe got up from the table, having stuffed himself to the point of pain, then smiled, the first real smile she'd seen come from his normally composed features, and, most unaccountably, he reached out to touch her upper arm. "I can only thank you for this breakfast, Mrs. Lukens. I can never really repay you."

Finally controlling her own wild flushing, Mrs. Lukens managed to murmur, "Very fine words, Mr. Conrad."

He thought so, too. Talking to a white person was so very different, requiring not only different words, but a different way of ordering one's thoughts. He didn't think he was doing badly at all.

And he had meant what he'd said. He found himself liking this red-faced, raw-boned white woman. There was good in her. He hated to think of her here on her own, so lonely. If she were one of The People, she would have their totality to fall back on. How could the whites leave their old ones so alone?

After saying goodbye to a beaming Mrs. Lukens, Gabe took his gear out to his horse, stowed it all, then rode on into the center of town, where he quickly located the big general store that he'd been told was here, which was the main reason he'd even bothered to enter the town.

Leaving his horse and gear tied outside where he could watch them through the store's front window, Gabe spent the next hour buying. He purchased blankets, traps, copper and brass pots, frying pans, coffee, hardtack, beans, a side of bacon, gunpowder, lead for molding bullets, and various other sundries. He discovered a hand-held brass cartridge reloading kit for the newer calibers. He bought very little actual ammunition, just a little for his own guns. He had little idea what caliber weapons he would find where he was going. Probably many ancient muzzle loaders.

When he had bought all he thought he would need, Gabe asked where he might purchase a pack horse. The store's owner told him where he could find the livery stable, and, leaving his little mountain of goods stacked up on the store's splintery floor, Gabe rode on down to the livery stable and bought an old nag that he figured would be just strong enough for the limited number of miles of travelling he'd need from it.

He returned to the store, where the proprietor helped him load his purchases onto the old pack horse. "Don't look like he's gonna make it too far," the store owner said. "Maybe we could load a few things on your other horse."

"No," Gabe replied curtly. "He stays as he is." He wondered at the man's foolishness. What kind of man would load down his fighting horse with too much unwieldy gear?

The transaction had been friendly, if somewhat impersonal so far, but now the storekeeper began to question Gabe. "How come so many things, mister? You got a little spread out there in the hills somewhere that you want to stock up? Hell, if it ain't too hard to reach, I can send a wagon out with your next order."

"No . . . just passing through," Gabe replied noncommittally.

A cunning look came over the storekeeper's face. "Now, I know it ain't any of my business, but in case, just in case, mind you, you're thinkin' of headin' out to do a little tradin' on the reservation, well, I know it's agin the law, but I got a little firewater stored away in the back room I could let you have real cheap. Lord knows them savages out there ain't got squat to trade, but for firewater, they'd trade their own mothers. Maybe their little sisters, too. I . . . ."

The storekeeper's voice trailed away as Gabe turned on him one of the coldest and most dangerous looks the man had ever received. "Anyone who sells whiskey to the Red Man should be shot," Gabe said in a voice to match the look.

In the face of that look, with sudden knowledge that this man was quite capable of killing him, the storekeeper could only nod his agreement, although Gabe knew that he did not understand. His own reasons for hating the sight of whiskey in the hands of The People, and the reasons the storekeeper and most other whites might fear to see it there, were quite different.

After paying, Gabe rode on out of town, the tired old pack

animal trailing along behind him at the end of a long lead rope. Gabe kept the pace down; no point in overworking the old nag. Soon enough its path would come to an end forever. Let it enjoy its last day or two. Let it enjoy the sun and the breeze and the blue bowl of the sky. Let it revel in the abundance that *Wakan Tanka* had lavished upon this beautiful land.

The day was indeed beautiful. The sky stretched away overhead, his view of it fringed by the delicate leaves of the lightly wooded country through which he was passing. It was warm, but not particularly hot, and the cool, fresh breeze blowing down out of the mountains lapped around him.

Gabe pulled off his slouch hat and stuffed it into a saddle-bag behind him. Now his long hair blew freely around his face, and he liked the sensuous feel of it against his skin. He wished he could take off these heavy, confining clothes and ride with most of his skin exposed to the sun and air, but he was not ready to do that yet; not when he might run into people at any time. He was still too close to the town.

He thought back to the days when there were no towns at all within hundreds of miles, when a man could ride for days without seeing another human being. When the only habitations were the temporary skin lodges of The People, which were not fixed permanently, but could be taken down and moved when the urge to see some other place arose within the hearts of their inhabitants. He remembered when the weight of human beings rested very lightly on the land. When it had not yet been disfigured by towns and the white man's trash.

Even though Gabe was reliving old memories, the vivid mental images passing through his mind in no way impaired his normal alertness. In the old days, in the world in which he had been brought up, anyone who let alertness slip, even for a little while, would not live to ride free for very long.

He first became aware of the danger as a vague sense of trouble, a tightening of the skin around his ears, a wordless feeling. He was ready, then, when from about two hundred yards ahead he heard a shot, followed by the high-pitched wailing of women. The kind of wailing that had filled his ears too many times for too many years.

The sounds were coming from the other side of a small rise located about a quarter mile away. Kicking his horse into a canter, with the pack horse having trouble keeping the pace behind him, he rode to the near side of the hill, then stopped before he could be seen from the other side.

Tying the pack horse to the lower limbs of a small tree, Gabe then rode forward just far enough so that only his head, half-hidden by leaves and branches, broke the skyline. He saw people below him. White men and native people. A dead, partially-skinned cow lay on the ground nearby.

There were five white men, apparently cowhands. And six of The People, an old man, a boy, two old women, and two much younger women. The old man was lying on the ground on his back. A dark stain on the front of his buckskin shirt suggested that he was wounded. The boy was down, too, but apparently only stunned, as if someone had hit him hard on the head.

One of the white men stood near the old man, possibly guarding him, grinning as three of the other men held down one of the young women, while another was dragging her buckskin dress up over her hips. She was struggling hard, but losing. From where he sat his horse, Gabe could see the black triangle between her legs quite clearly. The two old women were keening their terrible chant of mourning near the old man. The other young woman seemed to be caught in indecision, perhaps trying to decide whether she should attempt to escape, or remain and help the girl the men had pinned to the ground.

Gabe immediately spurred his horse over the hilltop, and came galloping down toward the people below. The cowboy near the old man either heard him coming, or saw movement, because he shouted to his companions, "Watch it, boys! Someone on the way!"

The men holding the girl looked up immediately, fear on their faces as if they expected to see a horde of wild Indians pounding down toward them. "Take it easy, Charlie," one of them called, out, visibly relaxing. "It's a white man."

Gabe pulled his horse to a stop about ten feet away from the men who were holding the girl. The man crouched between her legs had stopped hauling on her dress, but had one hand laid between her legs. Gabe could see his fingers moving. The girl was shuddering with either fear or disgust. Gabe decided that she could not have been more than about sixteen. "What are you doing to these people?" he asked curtly.

One of the men holding the girl stood up. "These here Injuns snuck off the reservation. Killed 'em a beef. We caught 'em red-handed. Figured we'd teach 'em a lesson . . . if it's any of your business, stranger."

Gabe pointed past the cowhands to the old man, who was trying to sit up, one hand pressed against his belly, from which blood was slowly oozing. "Is that part of your lesson?" Gabe asked quietly.

"Shit," the cowhand standing near the old man snorted. "The old bastard tried to attack us. Had to put a bullet into him."

Gabe saw no weapon near where the old man was lying. Nor did he see much point in reasoning with these men. From their accents, at least some of them were Texans, and to the average Texan neither blacks, Mexicans, nor Indians had any right to exist. Nevertheless, Gabe asked, "Did he make his attack before you started raping the girl? Or after?"

"Hey, mister," one of the cowhands near the girl snarled. "I don't like your mouth."

The old man was still struggling to sit up. Charlie, the man closest to him, reached his hand down toward his holstered pistol. "I think maybe I better put another one into him."

"If you do," Gabe said, just as quietly as before, "I'll kill you where you stand."

A ripple of tension passed through the white men. The ones clustered around the girl slowly stood up, then began to fan out around Gabe's horse. "What are you, mister?" one of them snarled. "An Injun lover?"

Gabe did not answer directly. "It is a beautiful day," he said softly. "Look at the sky, the tall grass. Feel the sun, taste the breeze. Don't you agree that it is all very beautiful?"

The men were confused by his words. "What the hell you talkin' about?" one of them snarled.

"I am saying that it is a good day, a beautiful day to die. Are you ready to die?"

The men were even more confused now. They had the drop on this meddler, they knew that. They had fanned out around him, two men on each side of his horse, only two or three yards away, with Charlie about another ten yards in front near the old man. They had him cold, but the son of a bitch's strange words, and the absolute confidence in his manner, made them hesitate. What did he know that they didn't?

Then the old man sat up. He stared at Gabe for several seconds, amazement showing in his eyes, and then he cried out in a piercing voice, uttering a few words in his own language, the words so distorted by the old man's pain and excitement, that no one understood them except Gabe.

Charlie, startled, whipped out his pistol and shot the old man in the chest. The force of the bullet's impact drove the old man flat onto his back again.

The other men, hearing the cry and the shot, pivoted toward Charlie, which gave Gabe the opportunity he'd been looking for. His right hand reached down, pulling the pistol from the holster on his hip, while his left hand crossed over to remove the other pistol from under his right arm. Spurring his horse forward, he shot left and right, his right hand pistol firing a split second before the other. One of the men on his right went down, shot in the face. One on the left took a bullet in the throat. The other two men immediately clawed for their guns, but Gabe's horse had already lunged forward, and when they fired, they both missed.

Gabe's plunging mount ran right over the man in front, Charlie, the one who'd shot the old man. Grunting from the shock, Charlie fell hard, his pistol spinning from his hand to fall near the old man. Once down, he did not move.

Gabe immediately spun his mount to the left, at the same time slipping off the far side, away from the remaining two cowhands, his left hand gripping the animal's mane, his left heel digging into the saddle. Both cowhands had recovered from their surprise by now, and were trying to get into position to shoot, but neither of them could see much more of Gabe than one foot and one hand, mighty small targets.

Firing from beneath his horse's neck, Gabe shot the man closest to him. He would have shot the other, but his horse, startled by the hot blast of the pistol so close to its flesh, shied away, and Gabe had to climb back up into the saddle to keep from dragging the horse down.

By then, there was nothing more to do. The boy, having regained some of his senses, had leaped up and tackled the last white man still on his feet. The women were right behind him, including the girl the men had been trying to rape, and while the boy was empty-handed, the women were not. Three of them had snatched up their skinning knives, and, pulling the man away from the boy, they began to slice and stab. The man screamed, writhed, struggled to squirm away, but within a few seconds they had stabbed him to death, and were still stabbing even after he'd stopped moving.

Gabe dismounted and went over to the old man, who, although badly wounded, was slowly crawling toward the gun Charlie had dropped when Gabe's horse ran him down. Gabe picked up the gun and handed it to the old man.

Meanwhile, Charlie was regaining consciousness. He sat up, groggy, and when his vision cleared, the first thing he saw was the old man, half-sitting, about five yards away, aiming the gun at him and weakly trying to pull back the hammer. "No!" Charlie whimpered, trying to crawl away backwards.

Gabe kicked Charlie's arms out from beneath him, so that he fell on his back. While he was struggling to sit up again, Gabe went over to the old man. "Let me help you, grandfather,'' he said, and reaching down, cocked the pistol for him.

Charlie was by now so terrified that he could barely move. He sat, propped up on his arms, staring into the muzzle of the cocked pistol, which the old man was aiming at him in a most wavering manner. Charlie looked desperately at Gabe. ''You cain't let him do this to me, mister,'' he pleaded. ''Hell, you're a white man just like me. You can't let some dirty Injun . . . .''

Blam! The gun fired, and Charlie screamed, but the old man's hand had not been steady enough and the bullet missed. The old man fumbled with the hammer again, and after a struggle, finally got it cocked. ''You cain't . . . you cain't!'' Charlie was screaming at Gabe . . . until the look of disgust in Gabe's eyes silenced him. ''It is simply your turn to die now. But why do you choose to die a coward?'' Gabe asked coldly.

Blam! This time the bullet hit Charlie in the forehead, blowing out the back of his head. Charlie flopped over onto his back, dead, his arms and legs twitching spasmodically.

The others were now moving toward the old man. He dropped the pistol, looked up at Gabe, then looked at the others, the four women, the boy. ''It is him,'' he told them weakly. ''I did not believe it at first, but without a doubt it is him.''

One of the old women knelt next to the old man. ''Who, my husband? Who is it?''

And then the old man called out, quietly this time, the words which he had shouted at the beginning of the fight. ''Don't you recognize him? It is Long Rider. He who used to live with the Oglala Bad Faces.''

CHAPTER FOUR

The old woman looked blank for a moment, so the old man continued. "Don't you remember, woman, the boy, the son of the white woman called Yellow Hair, who was Little Wound's woman, the one he took from the Whites? The boy gained his name when he had only fourteen summers, the year that the soldiers under their fighting chief, Reynolds, were on the warpath. The boy, this man, Long Rider, made his long ride through the snow, through the terrible cold, to warn us that the soldiers were coming."

The old woman looked more closely at Gabe, and then her rheumy old eyes lit up and she began to keen a high trilling sound of joy and excitement. "Come . . . come!" she cried out to the others. "A famous warrior has returned to us!"

Oblivious to anything else, the boy remained by the man he'd tackled, the one the women had knifed to death, striking his dead body again and again, counting coup, as was his right, since he had been the first to touch him.

But the other old woman and the two girls immediately came closer, to stare at Gabe. The old women began to talk excitedly about their memories of the old days, of the great warrior, Long Rider, the White Oglala. The eyes of the two younger women grew large, and they looked at Gabe with intense interest, woman without a man interest. Even the young boy began to pay attention, and came over to listen to tales of the old glory days, when the Lakota had been free, when they were the lords of the plains, controlling an area that stretched many days ride in all directions. No one noticed when the old man died, until the old woman who had been his wife looked over, saw his open staring eyes, and began to keen again, but this time it was the terrible cry of total bereavement, of death.

And of revenge. Picking up their skinning knives, the women began to hack at the corpses of the dead white men, while the boy scalped the one he'd tackled. Gabe stood to one side, watching, not taking part. At one time, years ago, he would have vied for the scalps, but for many years he had been uncomfortable with the idea of taking scalps, or otherwise mutilating those he killed. His time among the white men had made him see these activities, so natural to the red man, in a different way, in a way that made him feel somewhat revolted as he watched what was being done to the corpses.

He sat on a rock and reloaded his pistols. Finally the others' initial frenzy died away. He knew that to stop them prematurely would only have confused them, and he would soon have to confuse them very much anyway. He would have to save them from the future, something of which they thought very little, but rather, like their brethren, lived for the moment, for what was happening now. He would have to convince them that there was indeed a future, and that it would be an ugly future unless they began to plan for it. Something else he'd learned among the whites.

Judging his moment, he called them together. Attentively they stood around him in a group. The fact that he was a man would be enough to control the women, who naturally deferred to men. The boy, excited by his first scalp, and aware of being a male too, would have to be controlled by the fact that this newcomer was a famous warrior. As it was, they stood, ready for his words, the nature of which surprised them when Gabe finally began speaking.

"We have much to boast about in what we have done today," he said. There were answering grunts of excitement, and he thought for a moment that the women would start their long ululating chant of victory again, so he cut them off. "But we must never boast about this. You must never let anyone not of your own family hear the tale, nor tell it to anyone who might carry the story to the white people. For if they learn of it, if they learn that we killed these men, even though it was a fair fight, even though they killed one of our people, an old man, and were about to rape one of our women, it would not matter. All they would know is that we, The People, have killed some of their own, and they would complain to the soldier chiefs, and then soldiers would come in great numbers, to kill The People, not only the warriors, but also the women and children, and then they would burn the lodges and the food, so that any survivors would starve during the time of cold. So we must say nothing. Nothing at all that might reach the ears of even one white man."

They all stared at him, their faces showing confusion, mixed with a little anger. But he could see, particularly in the eyes of the older women, that the talk of soldiers had made an impact. They were no doubt remembering events in the past, ugly events, of soldiers attacking at first light, thundering down on a sleeping, unprepared camp, shooting, sabering, burning. For his own part, Gabe could not stop himself from remembering the same, remembering the deaths of his mother and his wife at the hands of those same soldiers. "Come . . . we have work to do," he said brusquely to the others, effectively cutting off his own memories.

They now followed him willingly enough, partly because his first suggestion was that they strip the dead whites. That they understood. It was an old custom, a right earned by combat, to strip dead enemies. Indeed, the opportunity of plunder had initiated many a fight.

But Gabe dampened some of their enthusiasm by checking

the dead men's personal gear, particularly the gunbelts, for peculiarities, such as initials, that would permit friends of the dead men to identify the equipment. Over the grumbling of the others, Gabe threw two of the gunbelts onto a small pile of items to be discarded.

He went through the same procedure with the horse gear, rejecting a fine saddle. He decided that the guns themselves must be kept at all costs; they were too valuable to discard. There were five pistols and three rifles. Three of the pistols were older cap and ball .44s, but there were two of the new Colt .44 metallic cartridge pistols, the same as Gabe himself carried. Two of the rifles were rimfire Henrys. One was a new Winchester .44–40. The men of the village would be happy to see such a haul.

Gabe had the women butcher the dead cow. But before they loaded the meat, he used the horses and the cowboys' lariats to drag the bodies of the dead white men over to a little gully beneath a cutbank. The bodies were then rolled down into the gully, with the two discarded gunbelts, and the one saddle, and the clothing and other personal gear piled on top of them. Then Gabe cut long pieces from several saplings for digging sticks, and with the help of the others, dug into the cutbank until they had collapsed it down on top of the bodies. Within an hour, the bodies, along with the discarded equipment, were completely hidden.

It required only another half-hour to build several travois for transporting the meat and other plunder. Saplings were cut for the long drag poles, with smaller limbs woven in between as lateral supports. The travois were attached to the horses, then loaded with meat . . . and the old man's body. Finally they were ready to go, everyone mounted now, as the Lakota were meant to be.

After an hour's ride, they found a secluded place for the old man's grave. They constructed a platform for him high up in a tree, and the old man was laid on it, on his back, the few possessions he'd had with him lying by his side. Gabe knew that the white men did their best to discourage this practice, that they had ordered the red men to bury their dead under the earth, as they themselves did. But the red men hated to think of their loved ones trapped deep in the earth, the moldy earth, far from the sun and the wind and the sky, preferring to know that the bodies were in the open, where birds would be able to find them, where they would be carried bit by bit by the birds and the wind and the rain to *Wakan Tanka*, up there, somewhere, in the vastness of the sky.

Afterward, they continued on toward the village, the old women bleeding a bit, having slashed their arms and breasts as a sign of their grief for the old man. Both appeared to have been his wives, although Gabe noticed that one, the somewhat older one, seemed much more bereaved than the other. Gabe guessed that they might be sisters, the old man having married the older one first, then the younger one when she became old enough, a common practice among The People.

They reached the village very late that afternoon, when the sun was nearly touching the hills far to the west. As the little cavalcade approached, still at a great enough distance so that few details could be made out, people came running out of their lodges, not knowing whether to be glad, or to be afraid, because the group that had left three days before had been on foot, and this group returning was not only mounted, but a white man was riding a little ahead of them.

Then the boy, yipping in triumph, galloped his horse forward, waving a handful of bloody scalps, shouting out the story of the great battle, and of his own bravery. Gabe winced, hoping there were no whites present, that the Indian agent was not making an inspection visit, or that white traders were not sitting in the lodges, bartering cheap goods for skins.

A quick look around showed no one but The People. Gabe immediately realized that they were a very unprosperous-looking group. The lodges were old and tattered; it had been many years since there had been buffalo to kill, buffalo to provide skins for new lodges. Gabe noticed two run-down old buggies parked near a grove of trees. There were few horses in sight, only a few sorry nags that would have trouble even with the lighter work of pulling the buggies.

And the people were haggard, thin, sick-looking. Quite a contrast to the old days, in which the men had been strong and muscular, the women sleek and lovely, everyone glowing with health, fed by rich stews of buffalo and deer and rabbit, which bubbled away all day in every lodge. But not here, not now. These were clearly a hungry people.

However, they immediately forgot their miseries as they listened eagerly to news of the fight, of the killing of enemies. And as the name of Long Rider sounded again and again, the men began to look with increasing excitement in Gabe's direction. At first they had thought him only another white man, but some began to recognize him. Women and children crowded around, although the men, not wanting to lose their dignity, stood back a little, until Gabe dismounted and came toward them.

A tall man in his fifties separated himself from the others. His face was calm and composed as he stood in front of Gabe, although Gabe could sense the excitement in him. "It is you, then, Long Rider," he said. "We had thought you were dead . . . like so many others."

"No . . . I still live. And you are Tall Bear. I remember you very well . . . from the time we fought the soldiers."

And now the man smiled openly, and his voice rose in exultation. "Yes, we fought the soldiers together many times. And now you bring us scalps and meat and horses and plunder!"

All restraint vanished as the entire village, about sixty people, crowded around those who had taken part in the fight, avid for details. The younger men among them, very few indeed, counted coup on the scalps, while the women trilled their delight.

Gabe quietly detached himself from the others, knowing that a very disagreeable task lay ahead of him, one the others would not understand, one they would even resent. While most of the people were gathered together sharing the victory, he walked over to where he had tethered the horses of the five dead white men. He hated this, he hated doing it, but it had to be done . . . before anyone could change his mind.

Drawing his revolver, Gabe shot one of the horses through the head. By the time the horse's body hit the ground, he had shot another. Then another.

By now the people were reacting, and several of the men ran in Gabe's direction, but by the time they reached him, he had already shot the last two animals. Tall Bear was so excited that he grabbed Gabe by the arm, a great rudeness, which Gabe pardoned because of the other man's obvious excitement. "What have you done?" Tall Bear demanded.

"I have shot the white mens' horses."

"I see that . . . I see that! But . . . why? Why destroy what we need so badly?"

"Think a moment, Tall Bear. Do you need death? Do you need destruction? Do you need the soldiers to come and kill your women and children? For that is what would happen if you'd kept these animals. Come . . . look! Here . . . and here!"

Gabe leaned down and pointed to the brand on the flank of one of the animals. Then he pointed to identical brands on the other dead horses. "See? They are all the same mark. A white man's mark. All the men we killed worked for a single ranch, they all rode the ranch's horses. If any of these horses were ever recognized, and connected to the dead men, and it would surely happen some day . . . then . . . you know the rest."

All the light faded from Tall Bear's face. "You are right, Long Rider. And that is what makes it so painful. We are now a people so weak, so helpless, that we must live in fear that other men will find out that we have fought back against those who kill us, who rape our women."

Tall Bear turned away a moment, and when he finally turned back, his voice was so low that Gabe could barely make out the words. "Surely," Tall Bear murmured, "it would have been better if we had been wiped out long ago, destroyed, so that we would not have lived to see our own shame."

CHAPTER FIVE

However, with all the meat from the butchered cow and the horses now available, it was impossible for Tall Bear and his people to remain despondent for long. Within half an hour of Gabe's arrival the women were cutting up meat and scraping hides. Large chunks of beef and horseflesh sizzled over fires, while stews bubbled away inside tipis. A mood of festival dominated the village, with little knots of people, thin people, sitting around fires, gorging themselves until the skin had stretched taut over bellies unfamiliar with being full.

Even then the women worked late into the night, by the light of large bonfires, cutting the leftover meat into thin strips and hanging it onto drying racks to cure over slow, smoky fires, so that it could be preserved to be eaten later. Some of it would be mixed with herbs and fat and berries, turning it into pemmican.

But while the women worked, Gabe went into Tall Bear's lodge with some of the leading men, the few that were left in this village of women and boys. Gabe was given the seat of honor, the *catku*, on the side of the lodge farthest from the door, next to Tall Bear himself. After the festival atmosphere of the feast, this was a much more solemn occasion. The men

sat quietly, no one saying much of anything while a ceremonial pipe was prepared. Tall Bear himself filled the pipe
with a mixture of tobacco and dried willow bark, *chanshasha*. Gabe felt a sense of familiarity and security steal over
him as he watched Tall Bear present the pipe to the West,
North, East, and South, the four directions, then hold it close
to the earth, and finally, raise it toward the sky. Tall Bear
then placed a coal in the pipe bowl, lighting the mixture, but
instead of smoking first, he passed the pipe to Gabe, to Long
Rider.

Appreciative of the honor, Gabe inhaled the pungent
smoke, feeling, as he did so, a sense of power entering into
his body with the smoke, a sense of unity with . . . With
what? Not a question that would have occurred to him before
he had begun to spend so much time among the white man.
Now his being was made up of disparate parts of two different
ways of looking at the world. It was confusing.

Enough. No more twisted white man's thinking. Tonight
he would be all Lakota, he would let the smoke increase his
personal power, and he would share that power among the
others who smoked with him, the men, the warriors of The
People.

Gabe passed the pipe to the next man, who smoked and
passed it on to the next, until the pipe had passed all the way
round the circle. Then the talk began. "We understand why
you had to shoot the horses," Tall Bear said gravely. "But
how we hated to lose them."

There was an answering murmur from the other men. Tall
Bear sighed. "I suppose we needed the meat even more than
live horses. Some of the children and the old people were
close to starvation. Another few days, and some would have
died."

"The hunting is bad?" Gabe asked.

"Haugh!" Tall Bear replied explosively. "What hunting?
We are squeezed onto this single miserable piece of land, the
only land the whites permit us. Our rifles are taken from us,
our horses, too . . . How are we to hunt? If there was any-

thing to hunt. The whites have killed all the buffalo around here, although I have been told that there are still a few animals up north. But can we go north? No, the soldiers would kill us if we left the reservation. We hunt a few deer and some rabbits, but even the deer are getting scarce. We have to travel a long distance to find them, but without horses it is difficult to travel far enough or get close enough to hunt with a bow. So . . . without rifles . . . ."

Gabe nodded. He was happy that he had been able to bring to the village the rifles of the dead cowhands. "If you take the saddles I brought you, and some of the other gear far to the east, away from the ranch where the white men who used to own them lived, you should be able to sell everything there without danger. Perhaps you can even trade them for another rifle or two. And I have brought powder and lead, and a device the white men use to make new cartridges, so your hunting will improve a little. But this hunger you tell me about . . . I've heard that the white man promised to supply the Lakota with food and other supplies in return for moving onto the reservation. Something they call an annuity."

A murmur of disgust moved around the circle of men. "They promised much," one man replied. "They promised to bring us cattle to replace the buffalo, and they do send a few now and then, but very few, not enough to feed the people, despite their promise of more."

Tall Bear broke in. "These promises," he said thoughtfully. "These promises that are broken. I have never understood why the white men even make the promises. Their soldiers have defeated us, have driven us from our land, they have won many victories. Yet they are still not content. Long ago, in the time of my grandfather's grandfather, we did the same to the Crow, driving them from the land they had held, the land that the Lakota were strong enough to make their own. We killed their warriors, raided their villages, took their women, even some of their children so that we might be even stronger, more numerous. We killed very many of the Crow, nearly wiped them out, drove them to the West, beyond the

mountains. That is the way of life. The Crow hate us, true,
and fought against us many times, side by side with the
whites. But that is the way the world is. We did not, after
defeating the Crow, after killing their people and driving them
from their land, promise to bring buffalo to them in the new
land to which they fled. Although, if we had promised the
way the whites promise, we would have kept our promise.
But still, I do not understand this promising. Why do the
whites, after defeating us, killing our people, taking our land,
make these promises?''

Gabe cleared his throat. ''It is a strange thing the white
men have, this way of thinking. They are very ruthless, but
when they do something ruthless, they feel what they call
guilt. They learn this guilt from reading a book, a very old
book about their god, a strange, dark, foreign god, one that
is apart from the sky, the earth, the stars, from everything
that is, a terrible god who separates the whites from their
mother, the earth, and encourages them to destroy the crea-
tures in it. Yet, and I know it will sound strange, it is this
book I mentioned, the book of their god, that gives them this
guilt when they do what the god tells them to do. And one
way they have of feeling better about this guilt is to go right
ahead and do something bad, something terrible, and then
pay money for it. To them, money, the yellow metal, is everything. They have a word for it . . . justification. They must
justify everything they do, not just do it. So, when they take
our land, they justify it later by making us sit down and put
our marks on one of their papers, a treaty, and then they
promise to pay us for what they took. But they never do.''

The men around the circle shook their heads in wonder.
''A strange people,'' Tall Bear said morosely. ''But with so
much power.''

Half-stifled sighs passed around the circle. Gabe, knowing
that this growing moroseness would eventually embarrass the
men, moved on to more concrete subjects. ''This annuity,
the beef and other things you are supposed to receive. How
are they delivered?''

Tall Bear snorted. "There is a man they call an agent. His name is Peebles. Other white men bring him the cattle. When he has collected a number of them, he has the cattle driven onto the reservation, where it is up to us to kill them."

One of the other men smiled. "We have a hunt then, or at least we play at hunting. We gather the cattle in an area and ride in among them, with out bows, or with the few guns we have, and kill them. But it's not really much of a hunt. And there are never enough to feed all The People. The food you have brought will keep many of us alive for longer than we had expected to live."

Although his face remained composed, as was expected, Gabe felt a rush of anger sweep over him. This once great people who had for so many generations roamed the plains, free, vitally alive, a people whose warriors were the best horsemen and hunters in the world, were now reduced to circling a herd of tame cattle, killing them in a parody of the old hunt. "And there are never enough?" he asked, his voice tight.

"Never. We starve," Tall Bear said simply.

"I will look into it. When I leave here, I will go see this Agent Peebles. I will ask him why there are not enough cattle."

The subject was abruptly dropped, and the conversation returned, with much more animation, to the old days, to the days of the hunt and of battle. Years ago Gabe had hunted and fought alongside some of the very men sitting with him at this fire. And alongside many more, now dead. So, for a few hours, the color and excitement of the old days existed once again, at least in the minds of these survivors. Tales were spun of surprise attacks against the Crow and the Pawnee, of stealing their horses, counting coup, taking their women, heroic tales of the Lakota, The People, the pirates of the plains, raiding, hunting, being raided. Tales of a life of constant vigilance, because to lose vigilance, whether it was the vigilance of the individual or the vigilance of the group, was to risk losing life itself. And once one had lived a life of such constant excitement, of constant conversation with survival, it was very difficult to sink into a life of inactivity and lack of movement.

Gabe slept that night in Tall Bear's lodge. It was not a crowded lodge; there was only Tall Bear himself and his one surviving wife. He stayed a week with Tall Bear's band. Shedding his white man's clothing, he dressed again in a breech clout, and riding out with some of the men, the others mounted on the few horses suitable for carrying riders, they were able, with the help of the new rifles, to bring back three deer.

Several times Gabe rode out alone, not to hunt, but to be alone with the land. Each time he came back to the village he found himself being appraised very openly by one of the girls whom he had rescued from the cowhands. Her name was Willow, and she was aptly named, being tall and slender, but also quite richly endowed with all that made a woman a woman. For a couple of days Gabe was circumspect with Willow, until he had ascertained that she was no man's woman, indeed, there were far too few men of the right age to go around; most had been killed in battle against white soldiers.

One afternoon Gabe found Willow looking at him with especially forthright invitation. There was nothing coy in her manner, in fact, she was much more aggressive than a Lakota girl should be. But these were changed times, the old ways had been weakened, new ways must be found.

So, when, after one last frank look, Willow turned and walked away toward a patch of woods about half a mile distant, Gabe bided his time for a while, then, when he felt a correct interval had passed, he leaped onto his horse's back and rode out of the village, not heading directly for the woods, but riding off at an angle, until a small gully, which hid him from the village, permitted him to change course for the wood and approach it unseen.

Willow was waiting for him as he rode in among the trees. She was sitting on a fallen tree trunk, erect, knees together, head slightly tilted down, but looking up at him with big, dark eyes.

Gabe dismounted and approached the girl, stopping a few

feet away from where she sat. "I cannot stay with The People," he said simply.

"I know," she replied just as simply. "But for me, today will be enough. We cannot hope that the old ways will come back."

When she stood up, he took her in his arms. Through the soft, beautifully tanned leather of her buckskin dress he could feel the heat of her body, the wonderful, strong pliability of her. Her breasts were large and firm, and they pressed solidly against his lower chest. Gabe and the girl held one another hesitantly for a moment, then Gabe broke away, returned to his horse, and removed the blanket he'd been using as a saddle.

While he was spreading the blanket out on the ground, Willow slipped her dress up over her head. Glancing to the side, Gabe saw her body emerge as the dress slid upward, first the long straight legs, then the dark patch between them, the slender incurve of belly, and finally the roundness of her breasts. She tossed the dress aside, then came toward him, naked, her eyes on his, her body straight and strong, as was normal with a woman who had grown up among a people who had for so long lived mostly on meat.

They stood for a moment looking at one another, each very still, as if waiting for something, and then Willow's loveliness, her beauty, the fact that she was here, for him, the dark shine of her eyes, the glossy black of her hair, overwhelmed Gabe. He tore away his breechclout, and they came together in a long shuddering embrace that echoed their terrible need. A moment later they were on the blanket, joining together with wild haste, the girl's thighs opening eagerly, the flesh near where they joined already shining with wetness. Almost immediately Gabe was inside her, felt her envelop him. Willow cried out once, just as he went into her, and then her back arched strongly, her arms tightening around him, and he could hear her breath panting into his ear.

It was quick, wild, necessary, and when they were both temporarily spent they still clung together, body to body. Finally Gabe rolled free and moved a little away from Willow so that he could more clearly look at her.

She smiled at him, her face soft, fulfilled. "It has been too long a time since . . . ."

"For me, too."

She looked surprised. "But you ride among the whites, and you have a white skin. There are so many of the white women. Tell me . . . how are they?"

He grimaced. "Cold. Not like a Lakota girl. To a white woman, their bodies are something to use for bartering, to trade for wealth or power, to control a man. Few seem to actually enjoy making love. The whites are very strange. Their god tells them that they must feel guilty about happiness of the body."

She smiled again. "You have made my body very happy today."

"And you mine."

They made love again, more slowly this time, savoring each movement, each sensation. Later they rode back to the village, openly together, Willow mounted behind Gabe. No one took any overt notice of them, although Gabe was aware of a few secret, pleased smiles.

However, good taste required that Gabe and Willow be discreet about their pleasure, and although they made love several more times, it was always out of sight of others, and always very pleasant.

It was the pleasure of it that prompted Gabe to finally leave the village. He knew that Willow would want him to stay, and so would the village itself. And the pleasure of what he and Willow had been doing together, the sweetness of it, would prompt him to stay. Which was what he could not do. The color of his skin and hair would see to that. The People would not object to his staying, but the white man would. No white man could live on a reservation without the consent of the Indian agent, and even if Gabe were able to gain that permission, he would never ask it from a man who functioned as The People's jailer.

And there were other reasons. The old life was over. He could never survive this newer, restricted life. He was a wanderer, he had grown up a wanderer, he needed space, he needed freedom, freedom to roam, freedom to pass over the face of the Earth as a free man was meant to do. And the one thing his white man's skin gave to him was the freedom to wander where he would, all over this vast land. Because of his skin and hair, he was free to leave the reservation. And that is what he would do, what he *must* do.

He made no proclamation, but everyone knew that he was about to leave. There was no overt attempt among any of The People to dissuade him from leaving, but he saw a little of the light go out of Willow's beautiful eyes, although she did not reproach him. Gabe took charge of the reproach all by himself, because he had already assimilated a little of the white man's curse of guilt. He had also picked up some of their practice of justification. So he promised, both to himself silently, and to The People verbally, that he was leaving so that he could go see the Indian agent, this man, Peebles, and enquire as to why there were not enough rations.

So he once again donned his white man's clothing, saddled and bridled his horse, and packed his gear. His pack horse he left with the village. He had originally intended to butcher it for meat for the village, but the unexpected windfall of the cowboys' horses had made that unnecessary. The old pack horse had been lucky; clearly, its time had not yet come.

The whole village came out to see him leave. Willow stood near the back of the group, looking a little sad at first, but then she smiled at Gabe, a smile of remembering wonderful things. There was no frown of regret, which poked sharply at that tender white place in Gabe's soul. And then the justification took over, and he vowed, took a terrible internal oath, that he would see to it that The People got the beef that the government had promised them, no matter what it took.

It was a warrior's promise.

CHAPTER SIX

The local Indian Agent was headquartered in the same town where Gabe had bought the supplies. Gabe made the return trip quickly, pausing only once, when he passed the place where the cowboys had been killed. Nothing showed, the blood had soaked into the grassy soil, and the cutbank effectively hid the bodies. If it had been up to him he would have left the bodies lying where they fell, as a warning to others. But he'd had the safety of The People to think of.

He reached town in the late afternoon. He quickly located the Indian Agent's office, and was relieved to see someone inside. Dismounting, he walked up onto the boardwalk and headed toward the door.

Inside the office a thin, reedy man, partly bald, dressed in Eastern town clothes, was seated behind a desk. Startled, he looked up when Gabe came in through the door; Gabe's soft moccasins had made no sound outside against the boardwalk. Standing with the light behind him, wearing his long linen duster and big slouch hat, with his hair fanning out beneath it, Gabe was a sight to give any man pause. "Yes?" said the man behind the desk, somewhat uncertainly.

"Mr. Peebles?"

"Yes." This was said with much more certainty, now that Peebles had been reassured by the sound of his own name.

"I've just been out to the reservation, Mr. Peebles. I found that the people out there have very little to eat. They were starving. Why is that?"

Peebles frowned. "You went out to the reservation?"

"Yes. I just said that."

"You should have checked with me first. White men are not permitted on the reservation, that's part of our treaty with the Indians."

"I went as a friend."

"You . . . . ." Peebles looked more closely at Gabe. "You a half-breed?"

Gabe felt a flush of anger. He didn't like the word half-breed, it fitted horses or cattle more than men. "No," he said curtly. "I'm full-blooded."

Peebles looked again at the light gray eyes, the long sandy-colored hair. Then he burst out laughing. "Oh . . . you mean full-blooded white."

Gabe didn't answer, just stood there, looking expressionlessly at Peebles, who began to grow nervous again. "Look, mister . . . . What did you say your name was?"

"I didn't say. And we're getting off the track. What I said when I came in here was that the people on the reservation are hungry. Starving. The treaty says that they're to receive ration annuities . . . beef, flour, tools. Where are those things?"

Peebles reacted huffily. "They get them. They get all you mentioned and more."

"That's not what I saw. They get a little, but not enough. Why don't they get enough, Mr. Peebles."

"Now see here . . . . ."

The agent's face flushed with anger. He wanted to tell this stranger to get the hell out of here, stop annoying him. But another look into those expressionless gray eyes, those strange, dangerous eyes, stopped him, and he became conciliatory, his tone now regretful. He sighed, a little theatrically. "Actually, you have a point, mister . . . ."

This time Gabe chose to answer. "Conrad. Gabe Conrad."

"Well, Mr. Conrad, the treaty with the Sioux and the Cheyenne does specify a certain amount of regular subsidy, and no man, believe me, Mr. Conrad, no man wants those poor people to get their full annuity more than I do. But I don't arrange for the annuities, I only distribute them, that is, when there's something to distribute. But you know how it can be, when it comes to the government. They promise a certain amount, they're full of promises, but they send less. Far less."

"Why?" The question was flat, remorseless.

The agent shrugged helplessly. "Perhaps a lack of allocated monies, perhaps chicanery among the suppliers. Some of the beef contractors the government has signed up, well . . . they aren't always the most honest of men, Mr. Conrad. God knows I've complained enough times to the head office back in Washington, but nothing ever seems to come of it. I receive vague replies, promises . . . . Nothing more, damned little beef."

"So, you don't receive all the supplies you are promised," Gabe said. "Some white man steals them before they get to you."

Peebles flinched. "A harsh word, Mr. Conrad. I prefer to think of it as confusion, bureaucratic confusion, perhaps mixed up with a little temptation. The human animal, you know."

Gabe's expression did not change, nor did he nod. "I think I'll look into this," he said flatly.

Peebles's expression changed again. The man had a very mobile face. Gabe was pretty sure that the latest change, lasting for just a fraction of a second, had been a look of alarm. "I don't think you should do that," Peebles said quickly.

"Why? If it's as you say, if people are stealing the goods that should come to you, then I'd think that you'd want it stopped."

There was another change of expression on Peebles's rather weak face. So far, none of the range of expressions had included honesty or strength. Gabe was getting the impression that this man Peebles, was slippery as a wet snake.

Now Peebles turned officious. "It's not the business of civilians, Mr. Conrad, to interfere in government business. As you know, or maybe you don't know, the War Department has charge of the reservations. I work for the War Department. We have our own means . . . ."

"Obviously not very effective means. Those people are hungry. A hungry belly can't wait for your . . . means. As I said, I'll look into this myself."

Peebles sat slightly hunched behind his desk, one hand on the desk. The other hand rose toward his mouth, then fell back into his lap. Now the look on his face turned to one of cunning. "Are you the man who bought all those goods for the Indians the other day?"

"I bought many things, yes."

"It's against the law to trade with the Indians without War Department permission, Mr. Conrad. You could get into a lot of trouble."

"Are you so sure that I was trading? Is it illegal to give things away?"

"It's illegal to disturb the savages . . . the Indians without official permission. Without permission from me. They're supposed to be secure from intrusion out there. They . . . ."

Gabe's voice lost the veneer of politeness he had so far forced into it. He walked forward and leaned his hands on the edge of Peebles's desk. Their faces were less than a yard apart, and Peebles felt himself trapped by those remorseless eyes. "I think I understand," Gabe said, his voice icy cold. "It's only illegal for the white man to enter the red man's land until the white man decides he wants more of that land for himself . . . despite what the treaties might say. I know that, and you know that, Mr. Peebles, so don't play word games with me. And as for disturbing the people who live on that reservation, few things are more disturbing than hunger, and that disturbs me too, a peoples' hunger. That's why I'm going to do all I can to find out about it, Mr. Peebles. Whether the War Department likes it or not.''

With that, he turned and walked out, leaving Peebles slumped at his desk, his head twisted to one side, where he had turned it to avoid those terrible eyes.

''Son of a bitch,'' he muttered to himself as he watched Gabe swing up into the saddle. ''That's all we need . . . a damned, meddling do-gooder.''

CHAPTER SEVEN

Gabe rode his horse back toward the town's one saloon, the one in which he'd had the encounter with the drunken cowhand. Looking in through the swinging doors he saw that the place was almost deserted. There were just a couple of seedy-looking old-timers inside, working hard at getting drunk.

Taking his rifles with him, Gabe went into the saloon. He had a strong aversion to alcohol, for what it could do to a man, for what he'd seen it do to so many of his Lakota warrior friends, but he also knew that alcohol could be a useful weapon . . . especially if one wanted to extract information. Fortunately, one of the men inside the bar was the town drunk and gossip. The approach was easy; Gabe simply sat down at the man's table and placed a full bottle of whiskey in front of him. ''I hate to drink alone,'' Gabe said, filling the man's glass.

As it turned out it was the other man who ended up drinking alone, although he didn't seem to mind, not as long as the whiskey kept flowing. Gabe filled his own glass once, but never touched it, all the while keeping up easy conversation while he refilled the drunk's glass again and again.

By the time the bottle was empty Gabe had solicited a good

deal of information, unfortunately a good deal of it concerning things in which he had no interest; the drunk rambled on and on. But within this flood of gabble were hidden a few interesting nuggets. According to the old man, a large shipment of beef allocated for the Indian annuities had been driven in two months earlier. ''Lots an' lots o' cows,'' he told Gabe. ''Driven in here by a real rich bastard, ole' Jason Brewer. He's got a big spread over in Eastern Montana. Not a very friendly cuss.'' Which probably meant that Jason Brewer had not seen fit to buy a drink for this gossipy old ruin.

Gabe sat toying with his full glass. Was this Jason Brewer the man who had been cheating the reservation out of its beef ration? Maybe he'd better go ask him.

Gabe sat for awhile, considering if he should spend the night at Mrs. Lukens's house, then start for Montana the next morning. Then he began to wonder if that was a good idea. As night fell, the saloon had begun to fill with men, just a few at first, then more and more as the day's work ended. Near the end of his talk with the drunk, Gabe had became aware that at least two of the newcomers were watching him with more than casual interest. He wondered if they might be some of the men who'd been with the cowhand he'd humiliated a few days before. But he did not recognize them. More interestingly, each time Gabe glanced in their direction, the two men looked hurriedly away, as if not wanting Gabe to know they were watching him.

Gabe immediately thought of Peebles. He had no doubt that he had made an enemy of Peebles, he'd realized it while still in the man's office. He'd apparently shaken something loose inside the agent. He'd definitely scared him. And while Peebles might be a weak man, he was also a man to be wary of. Peebles reminded Gabe of a rattlesnake, and he knew that there were few animals more deadly than a cornered rattler. It was time to start watching where he stepped.

Picking up his rifles, Gabe nodded to his drunken informant, who was by now hardly aware that he was there, and headed for the door. Out of the corner of his eye he noticed the two men who'd been watching him nod to each other, then get up from their table. As Gabe went out through the swinging doors, he saw both men moving rapidly toward the saloon's back door.

There'd be no bed at Mrs. Lukens's tonight; Gabe was not about to get trapped inside four walls in a hostile town. He rammed his rifles into their saddle scabbards, then leaped aboard his horse and kicked it into a fast canter toward the woods at the edge of town.

He had not quite made it to the woods when he heard the sound of two horses being run hard after him. Not bothering to look back, he vanished into the dark mass of the woods.

The two men on his tail plunged into the woods not far behind Gabe, intent on catching up to him. They had their orders—a few quick bullets and leave the bastard lying where he fell.

But once inside the inky blackness of the woods, they began to lose their confidence. "Where'n the hell did he go, Jim?" one asked the other. "I thought he was right ahead of us."

Jim pulled up his horse. "I dunno. Just sit still and shut up for a while. Maybe we can hear him."

Nothing. Not a sound. "Maybe the son of a bitch is just sitting out there, listenin' for us the way we're listenin' for him," Jim half-whispered. "Ya know, Harry, I got a feeling this ain't gonna be as easy as we figured. That gent looked like he could take care of hisself jus' fine."

It was a night of scattered clouds. The moon was half-full, but for the moment it had vanished behind a mass of cloud. The trail stretched away ahead of them, an inky opening hemmed in by the even darker mass of the trees on either side. Then they heard it, the sound of a horse's hooves about a hundred yards ahead, going away from them fast. "Come on, Jim," Harry hissed. "Let's ride the bastard down 'fore he knows we're on his tail."

Fifty yards later they hit the rope that Gabe had stretched across the trail, throat high, anchored to two good-sized trees.

Jim was riding just behind his partner when Harry and his horse hit the rope. The horse hit it first, the taut rope grazing its head, breaking its stride. Then the rope twanged back down, catching Harry high in the chest, slamming him down onto his mount's hind quarters. Jim's horse caromed into Harry's. Human curses mixed with the squeal of frightened horses, drowning out the swift drumbeat of hooves pounding back down the trail toward them.

Neither Jim nor Harry was aware of Gabe until he was nearly on top of them. The moon had by now slid from behind its cloud, and both men saw Gabe riding straight for them, rifle in hand. With each man fighting his mount, neither had time to react before the heavy barrel of Gabe's Sharps smashed them out of the saddle, first Harry, then Jim. Both men went down hard, and as they lay on the ground, bleeding and half-dazed, they were horrified by the ugly sound of the big rifle's hammer snicking back into full cock. "I'll ask you once, and once only," Gabe said icily. "Do you want to fight?"

"Hell no, mister," Jim blurted. "We jus' wanna go on home, peaceful like."

Gabe turned his head to one side and spat in disgust. "You can live, then. But tell the man who sent you after me to have the courage to come himself next time. I'll be back to see him soon."

Gabe put his rifle away and began retrieving his rope. While he was untying it from around the trees, Harry and Bill had a fine opportunity to open up on him, but neither man dared move, both remained lying where they had fallen, frozen with fear. This was obviously one hard-nosed bastard, one they had no intention of tangling with.

Gabe contemptuously turned his back on the two men and rode on down the trail. He had been tempted to kill them; killing cowards was worthwhile work. But he intended returning to this town, and a trail of dead bodies would make returning difficult.

He rode on another couple of hours, until a little after

midnight, he found a good place to camp. He'd spotted it from the main trail, a little rise that seemed to drop away on the far side. Riding over, he saw that he'd been right. On the other side of the hill the ground dipped down into a small depression, which was close enough to the hilltop so that he could easily keep the surrounding terrain in sight. A small stream ran by the bottom of the hill. He went down to the stream to water his horse, filled his water bag, then rode up over the hill into the depression, staked his horse well out of sight, spread out his blankets and bedded down for the night.

Before falling asleep Gabe considered the day's events. His instincts had immediately told him that Peebles was not a man to be trusted. Those instincts had been reinforced by the two men who'd been put onto his trail. Peebles obviously had something to hide. He was probably at least part of a plot to cheat The People out of their beef. In just what way, Gabe was not certain. Perhaps this rancher, Jason Brewer, would provide more information.

Information was what Gabe needed. He had thought of simply forcing Peebles to confess, then killing him. But that would not be enough. If Peebles was killed, another man like him would soon fill his place; Washington seemed to be full of such men. Probably always would be. No, the thing to do was show Peebles up for what he was, expose him, prove that he was cheating The People. That was what the white man always wanted . . . proof. That's what his Boston grandfather had tried to teach him, and his grandfather ought to know; he was a lawyer. Well, he'd get that proof, and by Peebles's example, scare off any future crooked agents . . . if someone didn't kill him first.

The trip to Brewer's ranch took almost a week. Gabe might have made it more quickly, but he found himself dallying in country he loved. His route took him through the Black Hills. This was where he had been conceived; his mother had told him that. The Black Hills had been sacred to The People. It had hurt very much when the white men took the hills for themselves. Only a few years before, one of the innumerable treaties had granted the Sioux and Cheyenne and Arapaho a vast area, made up of all of Western South Dakota and part of Montana, including the Black Hills, and the Powder river country to the west, up to the Bighorn Mountains. As usual, the treaty had granted the land forever, for as long as the rivers flowed, for as long as the wind blew.

Then the white man had decided to build railroads through the Powder River country, and worst of all, Yellow Hair Custer had pushed into the Black Hills in spite of the treaty, and discovered gold, the white man's obsession.

Naturally, with gold discovered, The People had lost the Black Hills, and the Powder River country too, but only after a bitter struggle, a full-scale war that had finally seen the death of Yellow Hair at the big fight on the Greasy Grass River, the river that the whites called the Little Big Horn.

Gabe had been involved in some of those fights, had ridden with Crazy Horse and Sitting Bull against General Crook. But courage had not been enough. The Red Men, with their minds caught permanently in the present moment, had not been able to plan ahead, to work together, and they had lost, lost badly, lost the Black Hills and the Powder River country, had been pushed onto the bleak lands of the reservations, lands so poor that not even the whites wanted them.

Gabe spent three days wandering through the Black Hills, awed, as always, by the lush valleys and jagged cliffs. There were still plenty of places where the whites had not yet settled, places to be alone with the land, to be one with the spirit that lived in the land.

Leaving the Black Hills, Gabe rode down toward the Rosebud River, where General Crook had been badly mauled by Crazy Horse. He passed through the Powder River country, where a treacherous attack by the army near the Tongue River, against the previously friendly Cheyenne, had brought them in on the fight against the whites.

Finally, Gabe found himself nearing Brewer's ranch, a vast expanse of land located in the shadow of the Big Horn mountains. Beautiful land. Gabe found himself admiring Brewer's judgment; the man knew how to choose good land.

The ranch headquarters was located near the base of some small hills. Gabe chose not to ride right in and confront Brewer. If Brewer was in on the plot with Peebles, riding straight in might mean certain death. It was a big ranch and had a lot of men working on it. They did not look like soft men, they could not be soft men in a country like this. They were all well-armed and looked quick.

Gabe camped out in the hills near the ranch headquarters. On his last trip East, he had purchased a pair of powerful naval night glasses, and now he used them to keep the ranch under observation. Each morning before dawn, with his horse hidden well back, he crawled to an observation point only a few hundred yards from the ranch buildings, making sure that he was safely in place before it grew light. Then he would spend the day observing the comings and goings below.

By the third day he was pretty sure he knew who Brewer was . . . the big man who so obviously gave orders to others. By the fifth day he had established that Brewer—if the big man was indeed Brewer—was in the habit of taking a ride in the late afternoon. He seemed to like to watch the sunset from a craggy hill about a mile from the house.

On the sixth day, Gabe rode to the hill himself. He met his man on the trail, about two hundred yards from the spot where Brewer usually watched the sun go down. Gabe more or less materialized out of the brush near the man, at a position where Brewer would have to pass by him to get back to the ranch, while a drop-off too steep for a horse lay on the far side of the hill, blocking Brewer's route in that direction.

Brewer stopped his horse and sat quietly, watching Gabe as he rode closer. Gabe noticed that Brewer showed no apparent fear, although he turned his horse a little so that it would be easy for him to cover Gabe if it came to shooting. Gabe respected him for that.

"Are you Jason Brewer?" Gabe asked quietly.

"Yep," Brewer replied. He continued to sit his horse without moving, but he never took his eyes off Gabe. He was, as Gabe had already noticed, a big man, perhaps in his early fifties. He was a little heavy, but appeared to be strong and active. "You know you're sittin' on private land," Brewer continued. "My land."

"I know. I came to see you."

"You could have ridden down to the house . . . asked for me."

"Perhaps. But I thought I should be careful."

Brewer's eyebrows rose. "Why?"

Gabe answered with another question. "Do you know a man named Peebles?"

"Peebles? The Indian agent? This has something to do with him?"

Brewer sounded surprised. But it was not the kind of surprise Gabe had been fishing for. "I have to know if you know him," Gabe persisted.

Brewer snorted. "Sure . . . I know him. Can't say I like him much. Did some business with him over in Dakota."

"You sold him some cattle for the reservation annuity."

"Yep. If it's any of your business."

"I would like to know how many cattle you sold him."

Brewer looked stonily at Gabe. "Well, now . . . I figure that ain't rightly none of your business at all, stranger. I might suggest that you just ride along and let me watch what the sun's doing."

"Very few cattle were delivered to the reservation," Gabe said. "That's why I want to know how many you sold to Peebles."

Sudden understanding now showed in Brewer's eyes. "What the hell? Is that slippery little snake sayin' I shorted him on the count?"

"Something like that, Mr. Brewer."

Now Brewer was very interested in continuing the conversation. He asked Gabe how many cattle had been delivered to the reservation. When Gabe told him, having gotten the count from Tall Bear, Brewer swore loudly. "Why . . . that's barely half of what I sold that little varmint."

"Peebles claims that he's consistently short-counted."

Now Brewer began to swear in earnest. "I never did trust that oily little creep. Slippery as a snake. And now he's trying to pass off . . . ."

He jerked his horse around, made as if to ride by Gabe. "Come along with me . . . down to the house. I got a bill of sale that says just how many head I turned over to Peebles. You can read it yourself."

When Gabe hesitated, Brewer testily demanded, "You can read, can't you?"

"I can read, Mr. Brewer."

But still Gabe hesitated, and then Brewer understood. "Of course. The bill of sale don't mean all that much on its own, does it. It could say that Peebles paid me such and such for so many cattle, but there could have been less cattle, and we could have split the extra money. Is that it?"

"That could be it."

"Well then, you can talk to the boys. They helped me herd those switch-tailed varmints all the way over to the reservation. They counted 'em so many mornings that they'll probably remember the number ten years from now. You look at the papers, then you just ask them."

Still Gabe held back. Brewer snorted. "Oh, hell, come on down, man. I ain't no back-shooter."

Gabe finally urged his horse forward. "I think I believe you, Mr. Brewer. Let's go down to the house and look at that bill of sale."

CHAPTER EIGHT

Gabe stayed two days at Jason's Brewer's ranch, partly because there were a lot of records to go over, partly because he liked the man.

The records, the bills of sale, and the information from the cowhands, were unequivocal; for more than a year Jason Brewer had been delivering cattle to Peebles in his role as Indian agent, far more cattle than Peebles had delivered to the reservation. Which confused Brewer. "What the hell's he doin' with 'em? That's pretty sparsely settled country. If he sold 'em outright, people would know. That many cattle don't just vanish into thin air."

"Wherever they went, I'll find them," Gabe replied grimly.

To give Gabe some ammunition to work with, Brewer took him into the nearest town, where he had copies of the various bills of sale notarized. "Shove these in the bastard's face. See what he says," Brewer growled. But when Gabe was finally ready to ride away to the east, he added, "Watch your back around that little four-flushin' bastard."

On his way back, Gabe stopped again in the Black Hills. Making camp, he spent an entire day and night sitting on top of a hill, lost somewhere in between thinking and meditation, laying plans. He had originally intended to take any proof of wrongdoing that he might get from Brewer straight to Peebles's superiors. But the more he thought about that course of action, the less attractive it seemed. How did he know that Peebles's superiors were not in on it themselves? The War Department, like most of the rest of the postwar government, was riddled with corruption.

The most important thing was to get food to The People. Perhaps he could use Brewer's documents to put a scare into Peebles, then force him to produce cattle for the reservation. The more he thought over this particular plan, the better he liked it. Besides, he wanted to face Peebles personally, see the fear in his eyes.

Feeling comfortable with this new plan, he rode back down out of the hills. They still loomed behind him when he noticed that his horse was limping. Dismounting, he found that a stone had lodged in between the animal's hoof and its metal shoe. He pried out the stone, but now the shoe was loose, but not so loose that he could easily remove it; the nails hung on stubbornly, embedded in the tough material of the hoof.

There was nothing to do but to try to nurse the horse along as far as he could. After two more hours, his horse was limping so badly that he had to get off and walk. He might have stopped right there, and done what he could with the bad shoe, but for the past couple of miles he had been passing scattered bunches of cattle. He was on somebody's ranch.

Topping a small rise, he saw the ranch buildings below, only a few hundred yards away. It was a small place, with two largish cabins and a barn, plus some corrals and smaller outbuildings. Small or not, they'd probably have some blacksmith tools with which he could repair the loose shoe.

He noticed that there were three saddled horses standing in the ranch yard, but he could not see their riders. Caution made him come up on the house slowly, still leading his horse. He tied the horse to a corral fence about fifty yards short of the house. He could hear voices from between the house and the barn, but before he started in that direction, the same caution as before prompted him to slip his Winchester from its saddle scabbard.

His moccasined feet making no noise at all, Gabe walked quietly around the corner of the house, then stopped. Ten feet away, three men, probably cowhands, were standing facing a young woman. Or rather, surrounding her. She had backed up against the house wall, while they'd fanned out around her. She was obviously not happy with the situation; she had an ax in her hands and a desperate look on her face. Her blouse was torn half away from her body, showing most of one bare breast and a good part of the other. "I'm warning you," she shouted at the men. "If you lay another hand on me, I'll see that every one of you hangs."

One of the men laughed. "Ah, hell, Kate. We'll just say you egged us on. A good-lookin' young gal like you, livin' out here all alone . . . . There's already talk in town."

The woman was trying to edge her way along the wall toward the door of the house, but one of the men moved in that direction, cutting her off. "I'm warning you," she said again. "The first man who comes close enough . . . I'll brain him with this ax."

The man who'd laughed before, laughed again. "Not if we take it away from you, Kate."

They began to close in on her. But unknown to the men, Gabe was closing in on them. Quietly cocking his rifle, he quickly aimed, then blew the heel off one man's boot, knocking him to the ground. The sound of the shot was deafening, and the two other men immediately spun toward Gabe, but he stepped in quickly. He did not bother to lever another round into the rifle's chamber, but instead swung the butt around and up, catching one man on the side of the jaw, sending him to join the other man already on the ground.

The third man reached for his pistol, but out of the corner of his eye he caught a glimpse of the woman swinging the ax down toward his head. He had no choice but to duck out of the way, and before he could recover, Gabe rapped his rifle barrel down hard against the man's wrist. The man yelped, and dropped his pistol.

The first man, the one whose boot heel Gabe had shot off, was sitting up, clawing for his pistol, so Gabe kicked him in the face, knocking him over backwards.

And now Gabe levered a round into the chamber, then tracked the muzzle of his rifle from man to man. "It doesn't matter to me whether I kill you or not," he said matter-of-factly. "I'll leave it up to you."

The men froze, partly because of Gabe, who was in front of them with the rifle, and partly because of the woman. She was standing right behind them, the ax still in her hands. And she did not sound happy. "Tell me, just tell me," she hissed, "why I shouldn't split your mangy skulls."

"Now look, lady . . . ." the cowhand who'd tried to draw on Gabe replied nervously. "We was only funnin'."

"Funnin'?" she demanded, looking down at her torn blouse. "Do you call this funnin'?" She let go of the ax with one hand, and tried to pull the blouse back up over her breasts, but when the ax nearly fell she let go of the blouse and it fell away again, this time completely baring the right one.

Gabe took time to notice that it was a very impressive breast, then he gestured toward the men with his rifle barrel. "I think it's time you left."

The cowhand with the sore wrist flared angrily at Gabe. "Who the hell do you think you are, mister, pokin' your nose into other people's business? That's a damned good way to get your head blowed off. If . . . ."

His voice died away as Gabe took a step toward him. "Men who attack women . . . ." Gabe said quietly, and from the look in his eye all three cowhands knew he was very close to killing them. Killing them not in anger, not with malice, but out of disgust, the way a man will grind into the ground something that he finds loathsome.

It was the woman who saved them. "No!" she called out sharply. "I'd like to see them get what they deserve, but I can't handle the trouble it'd cause. Just . . . run them out of here. Please.''

Gabe glanced over toward the woman, and her obvious distress made him decide not to start shooting. He looked back at the men, and his eyes, while no longer promising inevitable death, were not exactly reassuring. ''Get up,'' he said to the two men who were lying on the ground. The one whom he'd hit with his rifle butt was spitting shards of broken teeth. The other was bleeding from the nose and mouth. The one still standing had to help the others to their feet.

''Pick up your gun,'' he told the one he'd disarmed. The man was too surprised for a moment to respond, but then he bent to pick up his revolver, and it was not until he was actually holding the pistol, the butt filling his hand, the hammer near his thumb, that he began to get ideas. But one look into those expressionless gray eyes reminded him that he'd like to live at least a little while longer. He carefully holstered the pistol.

''Start walking toward your horses,'' Gabe said coldly. The men complied, walking ahead of him. After they'd swung up into the saddle, Gabe faced them for a moment. ''If we ever see each other again, I suggest you turn around and walk away. Otherwise I'll kill you where you stand.''

All three men swallowed hard, feeling fear and hatred welling up in their throats. But Gabe's very certainty, as he stood facing them, the promise of instant death, forced them to turn their horses and ride away.

Gabe did not even bother to watch them ride completely out of sight, but turned and walked toward the woman. He found her as he had left her, leaning tiredly on the ax handle. She looked up dully when she say him, and then, aware again of the condition of her clothing, let go of the ax handle and, using both hands, pulled the tattered remnants of her blouse back up over her breasts. ''I . . . well, I can only thank you,'' she said, somewhat shakily. ''You saved me from something that I think . . . could have been pretty bad.''

''Rape seems to be popular around these parts,'' Gabe said

bleakly, remembering the man who'd tried to rape the Oglala girl.

"Uh . . . what do you mean?"

"Nothing. Now, I think maybe you should go into the house. Change your clothes."

"Yes, I . . . ."

The woman had turned toward the door again, but had by now begun to shake so badly that she was having trouble walking. Gabe leaned his rifle against the house and took hold of her elbow, then had to put an arm around her waist to steady her. She leaned against him heavily, too shaken to be particularly careful of the ruined blouse, and Gabe felt his hand brush against the silky smoothness of her right breast. He carefully moved his hand out of the way. She was breathing unsteadily. "I . . . I think it's just a reaction to . . . to what they tried to do to me," she said shakily.

"It happens," Gabe replied. He guided her into the house, where he helped her sit down in a hard-backed chair next to a hand-hewn table. She bent forward for a few seconds, resting her head on her arms. Gabe could see her shuddering. When she finally raised her head again, Gabe was relieved to see that her face now looked calmer, but very, very tired.

Which was pretty much what she told him. "I'm tired of it all," she said in a quiet voice. "Tired of fighting to keep this place afloat, tired of fighting off Harrison, never knowing . . . tired of things like what just happened out there."

She looked down at her blouse again, and without bothering to pull it up, said, "Excuse me for a minute." Standing up, she walked toward the back of the room, where she stepped behind a blanket that screened off the rear part of the room from the front. Probably where she sleeps, Gabe figured. A couple of minutes later she returned, still fastening the top buttons of an untorn blouse.

She sat down opposite Gabe again, but this time stared off into space. Now that he had more leisure to study her, he saw that she was quite pretty. No, pretty was the wrong word. She was a handsome woman, almost beautiful. Probably if a man got to know her well enough she'd definitely be beautiful. She was a little above medium height, and remembering the shape of her breast, Gabe knew that she was very nicely built. Her hair was light brown, and shiny, as if she had just washed it. She wore it long, tied behind her neck, so that it hung halfway down her back. Gabe figured that she was in her middle to late twenties.

"Those men mentioned that you lived here alone," Gabe said. "I find that hard to believe. It seems to me that this is just too much place for one woman, for anyone, to handle alone."

She looked up, and a wry smile tugged at her lips, transforming her face, although the smile did not quite reach her eyes. "Are you making me an offer?"

He smiled back. He liked this woman. "I think you've had enough . . . offers, for one day."

Her smile faded. "That . . . bastard."

"Which one?" he asked, remembering that there had been only three men.

"Harrison," she replied bitterly. "I know he sent them; they were his men. He's been chipping away at me for a long time. First, he tried sweet talk, then he tried to scare me a little. This was meant to be . . . something I'd never be able to forget. As if I could forget that son of a . . . . Sorry. I guess I don't talk much like a lady. Maybe I just plain talk too much."

Gabe shook his head. He was very interested. He'd recognized the brand on the men's horses. It was the same brand as on the horses of the men he'd killed, the ones who'd shot the old man and tried to rape the girl. "This Harrison," he prompted. "Who is he?"

Her mouth grew bitter. "He's the man who killed my husband. Oh, he denies it, says it must have been rustlers, but I know he did it. He's wanted our land for a long time. He tried to get me to sell after Tom . . . died, offered me a ridiculously low price. As if I'd sell anyhow. This is . . . was, our land, and I mean to keep it . . . our land. Oh, I'm not really alone here. I've got an old Mexican helping me out, Juan, along with his wife and kids. They all went into town today to buy supplies. I'm glad he wasn't here. Juan would have tried to stop those men from hurting me, and they probably would have killed him. As it was . . . ."

She shuddered again, but her face was growing more and more composed. Gabe drew her out a little further, learning that her name was Katherine Miller. "Kate to my friends," she said. "And after what you did for me today, you certainly qualify as a friend."

She told him more about Harrison. "He's from Texas." Her lip curled. "Calls himself 'Colonel' Harrison. Sometimes I think all Texans with a little bit of money call themselves either 'Colonel' or 'Judge.' "

She told Gabe that Harrison owned most of the land in this part of the territory, or most of the really good land. Except for hers. She and her husband had chosen their land because it had good access to the best water for miles around. Which was undoubtedly why Harrison wanted it. "Or maybe just for the sake of getting it, of having more of something he's already got too much of," Kate said. "He's as greedy as a man can get."

When he figured that Kate had calmed down enough, Gabe asked her if she had any blacksmith tools. Jumping up from the table, she led him out to the barn. He liked the way her hips moved as she walked ahead of him, much the way Willow's hips had moved. This was not an ordinary white woman.

She watched while he pulled the nails from his horse's hooves, beat the horseshoe out flat, trimmed the hoof, then nailed the shoe back in place. He could have left then, but decided not to. He'd noticed the nervous way she kept looking out toward the brushline where it came close to the house, as if afraid that the three men who'd tried to rape her might come back. Not wanting to leave her alone, he waited until just before dark, when a wagon drawn by two mules pulled into sight. Kate and Gabe had been sitting out on the house's narrow front porch. "It's Juan," she said, relief in her voice.

She'd already told Gabe that she had been afraid for some time that Harrison might try to get at her through Juan and his family, hurt them, or drive them away, leaving her alone again.

When Juan got down from the wagon, he eyed Gabe warily. Gabe decided that it was the protective kind of wariness shown by a father when men start hanging around his daughter. Juan was probably in his sixties, a small, brown, very quick man. His wife was a lot younger than he was. They had a boy and a girl, the boy about ten, the girl a little older. Thinking of the type of men who'd been here earlier, Gabe was glad that the girl had been absent.

Gabe spent the night in the barn. He slept lightly, both rifles close at hand, in case the men tried a night raid. They'd been badly humiliated. Humiliated men will try foolish things. He was sorry that Kate had stopped him from killing them; they'd kill him now, if he gave them the chance.

He also slept lightly because of Kate. She fascinated him. He did not like being fascinated by women, especially by women who owned land, who were tied down, who might tie him down, restrict his ability to move freely. But, as he dozed, he could not stop certain images from moving lazily through his mind. Images of Kate's large dark eyes, the strong face, that bare breast. The way her hips moved when she walked. And most of all, her courage.

This Colonel Harrison. He sounded like a man who had no business living. A man who molested women. A greedy man, and of all the faults a man could have, Gabe despised greed the most, perhaps even more than cowardice.

When this thing with Peebles was over, he would have a talk with Harrison. A talk about the wisdom of leaving a certain young woman alone. That is, if he survived his business with Peebles. One never knew.

CHAPTER NINE

Partly as a means of ordering his own thoughts, Gabe left very early the next morning without seeing Kate. By noon he had arrived in town. Since his horse had been travelling hard over the past few days, his first stop was the livery stable. On his previous trip he'd noticed that the stable employed a boy about thirteen years old, who seemed to have a feeling for horses. Gabe paid the boy a dollar to rub his horse down, feed him some oats, put him in a stall, then saddle soap Gabe's horse gear.

As he was about to leave the stables, Gabe hesitated, wondering if he should take his rifles. He finally decided that he could trust the boy, so he left the rifles leaning in a corner along with the rest of his gear.

Gabe headed straight for Peebles's office. He was opposite the store when he saw two of the men who'd tried to rape Kate. For one lingering moment they shot a look of intense hatred in his direction, then, remembering his last words to them in Kate's ranch yard, his threat to kill them on sight, they prudently moved back into the store.

Peebles was in his office, seated behind his desk. Gabe

walked straight inside. "Don't you ever knock?" the agent asked irritably.

Gabe immediately answered Peebles's challenge. "I've been talking to a man, someone who had interesting things to say about you."

Peebles's eyebrows rose inquisitively. "Who might that be?"

"Jason Brewer."

Peebles's face stiffened. When he said nothing, Gabe tossed the papers Brewer had given him down onto his desk. "It seems that Mr. Brewer's been selling you a lot more government beef than you've been delivering to the reservation. A hell of a lot more. I want to know where those animals are, Peebles, because I intend to make certain that they get to where they belong. To the people who need them. You either send the animals themselves, or the money to buy more."

"You . . . you're . . . ," Brewer muttered, poking at the bills of sale. "I . . . don't know what the hell you're talking about."

"We both know what I'm talking about, Peebles. And unless the people out there on the reservation start getting some supplies fast, a lot of other people are going to know, too. There's a national election coming up soon. You know what that means; there are those who'd like to use something like this, a story about a corrupt Indian agent, to make a point. You could become a very expendable man. Maybe even a dead one. That I could promise you personally."

Peebles was breathing hard. Gray-faced, he made one last attempt to bluff it out. "These papers are fakes. You had them made up . . . ."

He was reaching a trembling hand for the bills of sale when Gabe scooped them up and shoved them back in the pocket of his duster. "We'll see if a federal judge thinks they're fakes. This isn't just a local mater, Peebles. It's national. You've been stealing U.S. Government property."

Peebles seemed to be getting himself under better control. His face hardened. "I admit, there may have been an occa-

sional miscount, but I assure you that there was no intent
to . . . ."

Gabe's face hardened too . . . with contempt. "Call it
whatever you want. Just so you start doing a better job of
counting . . . starting right now. If the people out at the reservation haven't received plenty of supplies, most of it beef,
within three days, then you're finished, Peebles. Understand?"

Peebles looked back at Gabe, obviously vacillating between hatred and fear. Gabe expected him to start either
shouting or whimpering, but to Gabe's surprise the agent's
manner became unctuous. "I suppose you have a point, Mr.
Conrad. I have been at the least . . . remiss in my duties.
You did right in bringing this to my attention. And I'll tell
you right now that everything will be taken care of immediately. Any past shortages will be made up . . . well within
that three days you mentioned."

Gabe nodded a bit dubiously, then turned and walked out
of the office. When he was out on the boardwalk he looked
back once. Peebles was standing behind his desk, leaning
forward a little, knuckles braced on the desk top, staring
intently at Gabe. When he noticed Gabe looking back, he
abruptly turned away.

Peebles's office was located on a short side street. As soon
as he was around the corner, and thus out of sight of the
office, Gabe stopped. He'd expected a lot more trouble from
Peebles. Gabe knew that he made a lot of men nervous, but
he was not so conceited that he was willing to believe that
the force of his own personality had been enough to make a
corrupt man like Peebles instantly see the light.

No. Peebles had given in too easily. As a matter of fact,
he had not expressly promised to deliver beef to the reservation. He had simply said that the matter would be taken
care of. There might be more than one way to do that, perhaps a way that would benefit neither The People, nor Gabe
himself.

On a hunch, Gabe quickly ducked into a narrow alley that

branched off from the main street. He chose a spot where a stack of crates further screened him from view, then settled down to wait.

It was a short wait. Within a couple of minutes Peebles went sailing by the mouth of the alley, walking fast, head down, elbows pumping, obviously a worried man, a man in a hurry. Gabe thought of stepping out into the street and following, but knew that he would probably be spotted; it wasn't a very big town, and out on the street he would have no cover.

However, since there was only a single row of buildings on this side of the street, it would be simple enough to walk along parallel to Peebles's route, behind the buildings, and keep pace with his quarry without being spotted.

Slipping along a series of smelly lanes, Gabe caught glimpses of Peebles each time the agent passed the mouth of another alley. Then came an alleyway in which Peebles did not appear. He must have stopped somewhere.

Gabe walked quickly up the alley, halting when he got to the place where the alley intersected the main street. A large stand of scraggly hollyhocks gave him cover as he peered around the corner. Gabe quickly pulled his head back out of sight. Peebles was standing only a few feet away, on the boardwalk, talking to three cowhands. The three whom he'd run off Kate's place.

"Is Dunn still out at the ranch?" he heard Peebles ask the men.

"Yeah. The boss's been keeping him on a leash. Ever since he . . . ."

"I don't want to know anything about that," Peebles said quickly. "You just ride on out there fast, and tell Colonel Harrison that we have problems. Big problems. Some stranger is poking his nose into our business."

"A stranger?"

"Yes. You may have seen him around town. A tall man wearing a slouch hat and a long duster."

There were muttered exclamations from a couple of the

men. "*That* bastard!" one of them finally burst out. "Oh, yeah . . . we seen him all right. He knocked out four of my teeth."

"Jesus," another said. "It's gonna be great to see Dunn make dog meat outta that son of a bitch."

"Then ride out now," Peebles snapped. "And tell the Colonel what I told you."

"Right."

There was a scuffing of boot heels against the boardwalk, followed by the sound of receding footsteps. Gabe heard Peebles sigh once, then he, too, walked away.

Gabe moved back down the alley, kicking at the dirt, interested that Peebles, pushed to the wall, had gone straight to Colonel Harrison's men, with a message for the Colonel himself. Which must mean that Harrison was somehow implicated in Peebles's cheating of the Indians. It would be interesting to find out just how.

Gabe walked back to the livery stable, where he sat down on a bail of hay while he watched the boy rub saddle soap into his rifle scabbards. "Do you know the Indian agent?" he asked the boy.

The boy looked up, smiling. He had reason to smile; this stranger had given him the very first silver dollar that he'd ever held in his hand. "Mr. Peebles? Sure. Kind of. He rents horses from us once in a while."

"How about Colonel Harrison, the rancher? Do you know him, too?"

The boy looked respectful. "Sure. Who doesn't? He's got the biggest spread around these parts. Supposed to have money comin' out his ears."

"Have you ever seen the two of them together? I mean, more than just passing each other by in the street."

The boy scratched his head with a leather-stained hand. "Well . . . I guess I seen 'em go into the saloon together a few times."

"They . . . drink together?"

The boy shrugged. "Gee, mister, I dunno. They don't let

me go into the saloon. Well,'' he added, grinning, ''not yet, anyhow.''

"So you have no idea what they might talk about when they're together?"

"Uh-uh. They sure as hell wouldn't tell a kid like me."

Gabe nodded. There were other places to find out about Peebles and Harrison. But first he should get himself something to eat. And maybe a bath. Probably the best place for both would be Mrs. Lukens's. He considered taking a room at her place for the night, but decided once again that he didn't want to be trapped within four walls inside a town where some of the more powerful elements seemed to be arrayed against him.

Walking through back alleys again, he made his way to Mrs. Lukens's place. Her face lit up when she answered the door, then her expression abruptly changed to one of concern. "Oh, dear, Mr. Conrad. I just rented out your room to a drummer from down Denver way."

Gabe smiled. "That's fine, Mrs. Lukens. I won't be spending the night, but I was wondering if there was any chance of a bath and some food."

"Why . . . of course."

He helped Mrs. Lukens heat the water on her big kitchen stove, then lug it out behind the house to the bathroom. A huge old claw-footed tin tub stood in the very center of the room. The wooden floor sloped away to a drain in the corner. A shelf held a stack of large clean towels, and a thick bar of homemade lye soap rested on a small stand next to the tub.

When the tub was full, Mrs. Lukens threw Gabe a quick, daring grin, then nearly ran from the room. Gabe smiled, then went over to the door and made sure that it was bolted, not against Mrs. Lukens, but against . . . surprise. More than one man he knew of had been killed while taking a bath.

He hung up his coat and slouch hat, took off his moccasins, and shrugged out of his shoulder rig and gunbelt. But while his pants and shirt ended up hanging on pegs next to his coat, both pistols plus the knife travelled with him to the tub. He placed the weapons on the floor next to the tub. If they got wet he could dry them later. But if he needed them in a hurry and they weren't in easy reach, there might not be any later.

Gabe caught his breath as he slipped down into the tub. The water was *hot*! But his skin soon got used to the temperature, and now the heat was able to reach deep into his muscles and bones. Gabe loved baths, he loved being clean. His life amongst the Lakota had gotten him used to bathing; the Lakota, like most Indians, bathed frequently. He'd never quite gotten used to the stench so prevalent among the unwashed whites, who, for the most part, thought that taking baths was bad for the health. Gabe had grown up bathing naked in streams, even as a child, even in winter . . . if the ice was not too thick. Later, when he was older, to counteract the cold there had been the sweat lodge for cleansing, the stream for washing.

He lay in the bath for an hour. The tub was deep enough, could hold enough, so that the water retained its heat for a long time. Finally, when the water was beginning to feel clammy, he got out of the tub, dried himself, dressed, and headed into the house.

Once again the kitchen was redolent with the good smells of Mrs. Lukens's cooking. Within five minutes Gabe was tucking into fried chicken, homemade biscuits, beans, and some cooked spinach greens. After coffee, he had to shake his head when Mrs. Lukens offered him a second piece of fresh-baked berry pie. "Mrs. Lukens," he protested, "if I eat another bite my horse'll never be able to carry me. Even if I could get on him."

"You're riding out for sure, then," she said, sounding disappointed.

"Later tonight."

He did not add that it would be after he'd poked around a little more. He'd asked Mrs. Lukens about any possible connection between Peebles and Harrison, but she had professed complete ignorance. "I pretty much stick around the place,

Mr. Conrad. What goes on in the town don't make much mind to me.''

After parting with another dollar and a half, Gabe finally managed to pry himself loose. He stopped by the livery stable. The boy was dozing on a stack of hay, but leaped up when Gabe came in. Gabe tossed the boy fifty cents. "I'd appreciate it if you'd saddle and bridle my horse in about half an hour. Go ahead and put all my gear on him, the saddle bags, the rifles, everything. I'll want to be riding out before dark."

The boy looked curious. For just a moment he wondered if this stranger intended to rob the bank, then light out fast. But the half-dollar interested him far more than the possibility of a bank robbery. He promised Gabe that his horse would be waiting the moment he showed up.

Gabe walked quickly down the street, heading toward the saloon. He was relieved when he did not see any of the men he'd run off from Kate's. He was also relieved, on entering the saloon, to see the same old drunk who'd given him the information about Brewer. He was half-slumped at his usual table, an empty glass in front of him. The glass looked like it had been empty a long time. The old man sensed Gabe standing next to him. He looked up. His rheumy eyes had trouble focusing at first, then they brightened with hope when he recognized his benefactor. "Well," he rasped. "Set awhile, stranger."

Gabe nodded, then went over to the bar for a bottle. He could feel the old man's hopeful eyes on him all the way, although, when he headed back, the old man was looking studiously down at his empty glass . . . which Gabe filled even before he sat down.

He took it easy, like the first time, waiting until the old man had put away a couple of glasses of whiskey. The old timer seemed as talkative as ever . . . until Gabe started asking questions about Colonel Harrison, then he clammed up, and when Gabe persisted, growled, "That's one gent it ain't safe to get on the bad side of. Big man in these parts. Got cattle and land out the ears.''

Gabe grunted assent, then fell silent for a moment. ''Seems kinda strange then, that a big man like Harrison would go runnin' around after a little man like Peebles, the Indian agent.''

The old man snorted derisively. ''You got it the wrong way 'round, Mister. It's Peebles who goes sniffin' around after Harrison. What they got goin' together I ain't sure, but I'd bet a barrel o' whiskey that it ain't . . . .''

The old drunk's voice trailed away. Gabe noticed that he was staring toward the saloon's swinging door. Gabe followed his gaze, and saw, standing just inside the doorway, the three men who'd tried to rape Kate, along with a fourth man. All four of them were staring at Gabe. ''Oh, God,'' the old man murmured. ''I kin smell trouble comin'. See that gent over there by the door?''

He obviously meant the newcomer. Gabe nodded. ''I don't know what kinda hassles you been gettin' yourself into, mister, but me, I'm lightin' out. That there man's Sam Dunn, Colonel Harrison's hired killer.''

CHAPTER TEN

Gabe was aware of other men clustered on the boardwalk around the doorway; there seemed to be at least a dozen. The swinging doors began to push inward, but a man already inside, one of the men Gabe had humiliated earlier at Kate's place, turned and snarled, "Keep outta this. It's between him an' us."

The doors swung shut, although Gabe was aware of a face or two still peering inside. But he knew he must not let the men on the boardwalk distract him. The four men already inside the saloon were now moving deeper into the room, the one the old man had called Dunn leading them over toward the bar. Every step of the way Dunn's eyes never left Gabe, stayed fastened on him malevolently.

Gabe pushed his chair back from the table, but did not yet stand up. The old man, snatching the nearly empty whiskey bottle, muttered something unintelligible, staggered to his feet, then scuttled toward the rear of the room.

Gabe leaned forward, with his elbows resting on the table-top, apparently relaxed, but with his left hand conveniently close to the butt of the pistol hidden beneath his right armpit. He locked eyes with Dunn.

Dunn placed his left elbow on the bar, also apparently relaxed, but Gabe noticed that his feet were still planted firmly on the floor, and his right hand hovered near the pistol that he wore on his right hip. Gabe and Dunn continued to hold one another's gaze, the eyes of each man somewhat hooded and sleepy-looking, yet unblinking. Finally Dunn broke the silence. "Your name Conrad?"

Gabe studied the other man for several seconds before answering. Dunn was of average size, well-built, on the lean side, and handsome in a disturbingly feral way. His voice was somewhat higher and thinner than Gabe would have expected, although the voice fitted his eyes, which were a faded light blue, with no depth to them at all. The man is crazy, Gabe thought, vicious crazy. A man who liked inflicting pain and death.

"Yes . . . my name is Conrad," Gabe finally replied. He still had not moved, but his eyes were studying the disposition of the three men who'd come in with Dunn. The bar was to Dunn's left, with the doorway to his right. The three other men were strung out to Dunn's right, in a slightly curving line. The more Gabe studied them, the less they looked like ordinary cowhands. More like men who lived by violence and theft. They were all smiling wolfishly, and Gabe knew how much they wanted to kill him. Four against one. Bad odds. If they all went for him at once, he was unlikely to survive. He could only hope that the three on Dunn's right would wait for Dunn to make his move first.

"I hear you're an asshole," Dunn said casually. The men with him snickered.

"I hear your name's Sam Dunn," Gabe replied. "Which, I suppose, amounts to the same thing."

Dunn had been smiling slightly. Now the smile vanished from his face. A slight tic started to pulse next to his right eye. "I'm gonna kill you for that, Conrad," he said, his voice ugly. "But I'll give you a choice. Do you want to take it standing? Or sitting?"

Dunn moved away from the bar, took the gunfighter's

stance, legs slightly bent, arms crooked, right hand close to his gun butt. "I think I'll take it standing," Gabe replied calmly.

He carefully stood up. His only visible weapon was the pistol holstered on his right hip, butt forward, cavalry style. He carefully kept his right hand away from it. It was important not to make any threatening moves. Not yet. He'd had a few minutes to study his opponent, and had decided that he was the kind of killer who needed to pump up his own ego before pulling the trigger. It would be important to keep him talking, to keep the initial part of the fight between himself and Dunn.

Dunn helped him a little. The other three men had begun to strain forward, hands drifting down toward their gunbutts. Dunn shot a quick look in their direction. "Hold it," he snarled. "First shot goes to me. When I've got one or two in the bastard, then you can shoot him up all you want."

Dunn's eyes flicked back to Gabe, not that his attention had ever completely wavered. Gabe remained standing in the most unthreatening posture he could manage, the thumb of his left hand hooked casually in his gunbelt, his right hand held up in front of him, away from his body.

Dunn immediately noticed his crippled index finger, the trigger finger, with its lower joint bent out at a nearly ninety degree angle, and like so many other men, he immediately assumed that the deformity would make it difficult for Gabe to handle a gun quickly. Dunn smiled, relaxed a little. "Hate to take advantage of a cripple," he said, although his tone said otherwise.

"Then maybe we should just forget about this. Go our own ways."

Gabe was still standing as before, right hand a little out in front of him, pointing in Dunn's direction, almost as if it were meant to hold Dunn off. The gesture of a man who is afraid, who does not want to fight.

And then Dunn gave him what he wanted, continued to talk, and in Gabe's experience, men like Dunn, men who needed to talk before they acted, were unlikely to make their move before they'd finished their sentence.

"Can't do that, Conrad," Dunn said. "You've been making waves . . . bothering friends of . . . ."

Seeing that Dunn was now fully committed to his closing speech, Gabe made his move. But not with his right hand. His outstretched right effectively screened his left hand, as it moved, without haste, cross-body, to reach beneath the right lapel of his duster and draw the pistol he wore in his shoulder holster.

It was an easy move, seemingly without hostile intent, so that Dunn was still gaping as Gabe pulled the hammer back. Dunn moved then, his body hunching, his right hand streaking down toward his pistol. He was fast, incredibly fast, Gabe had to give him that, but Gabe was too far ahead of him, and he shot Dunn through the chest before the other man's pistol cleared leather.

There were the other three men, of course, and even as Dunn was flying backward under the impact of the heavy forty-four caliber slug, they were reaching for their own pistols.

Which Gabe had expected. Twisting his body toward them, he reached out with his right, laying his fingers over his left hand, which gripped the butt of the pistol. Holding the trigger back with his left index finger, he began fanning the hammer with the thumb of his left hand, spraying bullets at the three remaining men. It was a much more accurate procedure than the way most men fanned a pistol, simply slamming the edge of their hand against the hammer. With both hands wrapped around the gunbutt, steadying the pistol, making it easier to control the recoil, Gabe could both fire at high speed, and direct his bullets with considerable accuracy.

He went right down the line of men, pumping a bullet into each, then adding a bullet to two of the men who were still showing signs of fight. It was all over in less than ten seconds, from the bullet that went into Dunn, to the final bullet that slammed the last of the stunned gunmen back against the saloon wall.

Gabe slipped the smoking, empty pistol back into its shoulder holster, then drew the other pistol with his right hand. Dunn had been lying on the floor, a patch of blood slowly spreading over his chest. Now he started to sit up, groaning in pain. Gabe noticed that Dunn still held his pistol, so he shot him through the head. Dunn went over onto his back again, his legs jerking convulsively, the way a chicken twitches after its head has been cut off. There would be no more danger from Sam Dunn. Not ever.

Gabe swept his pistol over the prostrate bodies of the other three gunmen. None was moving, which was good enough for Gabe. He heard disbelieving cries from outside on the boardwalk, saw faces crowding the doorway, heard the thunder of bootheels approaching from further away. How many Harrison men were out there, anyhow?

Glancing around the bar, Gabe saw no one there who looked like an immediate threat, so he turned and walked quickly toward the back door. One man took a half-step toward him, but when Gabe shifted the muzzle of his pistol in that direction the man shook his head hurriedly, partially raised his hands, and backed away.

Glancing back at the doorway, Gabe saw the doors begin to bulge open. He snapped a shot into the door frame. There were curses from outside, and the door swung shut again, but Gabe knew that happy situation would not continue for long, so he stepped out the back door into an alley. Barely in time. He heard the saloon's double doors slam open, heard men rushing inside. "Jesus!" one man shouted. "He got 'em all! Even Dunn!"

"He ran out the back way," another voice, high-pitched with tension, called out. Gabe bet himself that it was the man who'd made that half-hearted move against him on his way out. Not that it mattered. What mattered was that he get the hell out of here. He was clearly in an enemy town, one owned by Harrison, and by extension, Peebles.

The saloon's back door crashed open and a man appeared silhouetted in the doorway. Gabe saw the gleam of a pistol in the man's hand, so he fired, not trying to hit the man himself, but rather sending the bullet into the door frame, where it sprayed splinters into the gunman's face. "Jesus!" he bellowed, ducking back inside.

"He's still in the alley," another voice shouted from inside the barroom. "Let's get around to the sides, pin him down before he gets away."

That was a thought that had already occurred to Gabe, both getting away, plus the danger of finding himself trapped from either end. He began to run down the alley in the direction of the stables. He had already stuffed the partially loaded pistol into its holster, then pulled the other one from the shoulder rig, and as he ran, he quickly ejected the empties and began stuffing new cartridges into the chambers. He hated empty guns, hated being undergunned, too and cursed himself for leaving the rifles with his horse.

There were shouts from behind him. "There he goes!" one man yelled. Guns crashed. Bullets whacked into nearby walls, plowed up dirt ahead of Gabe, but he was not too concerned, not yet. It was a dark night, hitting him would not be easy.

He had almost reached the mouth of the alley when he saw dark figures ahead. Damn! They'd already circled around. "That's him!" someone shouted.

Gabe ducked to his right. Just in time. Guns spat fire and lead at him from the mouth of the alley. He slipped behind a small outbuilding, temporarily disappearing from view, which emboldened his pursuers to come on fast.

So far Gabe had tried to avoid killing anyone else, not sure whether he'd be shooting honest citizens or Harrison thugs. Now he had no choice, not if he wanted to live. Suddenly stepping out from behind the outbuilding, he surprised half a dozen men running in his direction. They tried to stop as Gabe fanned a full cylinder into the midst of them. One cried out in pain and clutched his belly, another two went down hard. The survivors turned and ran for cover.

Moving silently thanks to his moccasins, Gabe ran on toward the stables. But by now his pursuers had a pretty good idea of the direction in which he was headed, and came pounding along after him, so close behind that Gabe made it to the stables only slightly ahead of them. He burst in through the side door, gun in hand, eyes sweeping around the room. The first thing he noticed was the boy, who, having heard the shooting, was standing flattened against the rear wall, his eyes huge. Then Gabe saw that the boy had done as he'd paid him to do . . . saddled his horse and stowed his gear.

"Thanks, son," Gabe panted. The boy nodded, afraid to move. Gabe jerked the reins free from where they'd been tied, vaulted up into the saddle, and, using the rein ends as a quirt, lashed his horse into a dead run straight toward the open stable doors.

He was pulling his Winchester from its saddle scabbard even before his mount reached the doors. With the reins now looped over the saddle horn, and guiding his horse with pressure from his knees, Gabe levered a round into the chamber and came out of the stable shooting. There were already men closing in. One went down immediately, others scattered for cover. Gabe rode right through them, firing to both left and right.

The only way out of town was straight down the main street. Leaning close to his horse's neck, Gabe rode on, hard. There were still men in front of the saloon. Men with guns. Gabe poured fire in among them, not trying to hit individual targets, but rather hoping to scatter them, force them to take cover, so that they would not be able to fire back.

It worked. Most of the men ducked back inside the saloon. Seeing that the way ahead looked clear, Gabe let out a whoop of joy, a sound from the old days, and rode on out of town into the woods.

CHAPTER ELEVEN

Gabe had barely ridden into the woods when he heard the thunder of hoofbeats behind him. The Rocking H men had lost no time at all in mounting a pursuit. From the sounds they made, there were a hell of a lot of them.

Gabe's first reaction was to head in the direction in which he'd ridden before . . . toward the reservation. Except that he had no wish to lead this mob of vengeful white men down onto The People. So, where the trail branched, he headed more to the north than he had before.

For a couple of hours all went well. This particular branch of the trail led toward the Badlands, a rugged, uninhabited area in which he figured it would be easy to lose himself. Unfortunately, he was not at all familiar with his present route, and about an hour before dawn, he became aware that the trail had begun to descend into a steep-sided canyon, with walls so sheer he had no choice but to go straight ahead. Which made him nervous. He hated having no options.

On the plus side, the men following him seemed to have fallen further and further behind, part of which Gabe attributed to the superior strength of his horse. He'd been pushing

the animal hard, but now, with pursuit further behind, he
began to slow the pace. His mount was clearly tiring.

Just after dawn, he reached the lower mouth of the canyon,
where other, shallower canyons, ran into it from either side.
He was debating which way to turn when he suddenly became
aware of movement from further up the canyon to his right.
For a moment he thought that it might be a small herd of
deer or elk, but quickly realized that he was looking at
mounted men. His next thought, a hope, actually, was that
they were a party of prospectors or hunters, but when the
men were about half a mile away, one of them rose up in his
stirrups, pointed at Gabe, and shouted to the others.

It was the Rocking H men. Somehow they had gotten
around in front of him, perhaps using a short cut that he knew
nothing about. They'd no doubt realized that he was committed to continuing up this canyon, and had acted accord-
ingly.

Gabe spent several seconds deciding what to do. The land
ahead of him stretched away fairly flat. But if he headed in
that direction he doubted that his tired mount would be able
to keep him far enough ahead of his pursuers. They'd eventually run him down, and in such open land there would not
be many places to hide or to slip away. There were about
twenty men in the posse, too many to fight out in the open.

So he let them drive him up the canyon that lay to his left,
hoping that they would not have some other way of getting
around him. As he rode, still doing his best to save his horse,
Gabe looked for some means of slipping away to the side
without being seen, but none appeared. He was as locked in
as before.

Finally, about three in the afternoon, with the posse having
closed the distance a little, and his horse blowing hard, Gabe
knew that he would have to make a stand.

He didn't have as much time as he would have liked to
choose his spot, but he finally decided on a hillock that rose
up more or less in the center of the canyon, which by now
had narrowed considerably. He guided his horse into an area

of boulders, where it would be sheltered. Dismounting, he took both of his rifles, walked to the downslope edge of the hillock, then settled himself behind some smaller rocks.

From here, he could see quite a distance down the canyon. The riders were now only about a quarter mile away, somewhat below Gabe on fairly open ground. Knowing he had very little time, Gabe quickly raised the Sharps's adjustable rear sight, set the crossbar for four hundred yards, cranked back the big hammer, and aimed, not at any of the riders, but at the leading horse.

Kaboom! The roar of the big rifle reverberated from the canyon walls. A big cloud of white smoke burst from the muzzle, billowing ten yards ahead, obscuring Gabe's view for a moment, but as it cleared, he saw that the horse he'd aimed at had gone down, pitching its rider onto the ground.

Gabe moved the hammer back to half-cock, flipped open the action, and slipped another of the huge cartridges into the chamber. Once again it was cock, aim, fire. Another horse went down.

By now his pursuers had come to a halt. Even among the racket of their confusion they could hear, coming from the rocks up ahead, the ominous clacking of another round being fed into the Sharps's chamber. They'd already learned that their quarry could shoot quite well, so, as a third shot boomed out and another horse went down, the men still mounted pulled the fallen riders up behind them and raced away toward the nearest cover, a few hundred yards further down the canyon.

For the next two hours, it was a standoff. No one among the posse was armed with a rifle anywhere near the caliber of Gabe's Sharps. He was able to force them to keep their heads down, chipping stone from their cover whenever a man was careless enough to show himself. They were unable to reach him with their saddle guns, which were mostly Winchester lever actions, firing what were, in effect, pistol cartridges.

Meanwhile, Gabe's horse was getting a much-needed rest,

able to graze on the canyon's meager grass. Twice Gabe
crawled back to where the animal was tied, giving it water
from his canteen. He figured that if he could maintain the
standoff until a little after dark he would have a chance of
riding out quietly, and maybe gaining some time to lengthen
his lead.

Fortunately, he did not grow complacent. When he heard
the sounds behind him—the scrape of a boot against loose
stone, the clink of a weapon—he was able to react instantly.
Three men appeared out of a small gully to his rear—they'd
obviously cut around to the side without his seeing them, with
the obvious object of bushwacking him from behind.

When Gabe spotted the men, they were only about forty
yards away, moving cautiously from their cover out into the
open. They saw him at the same moment, and slapping their
rifles to their shoulders, opened fire.

Letting the Sharps drop, Gabe snatched up his Winchester
and rolled to one side. Bullets struck the ground where he'd
been lying a moment before. As he came out of the roll, he
sprang to his feet, and, firing from the hip, shot one of the
men in the leg, knocking him off his feet.

Then he was hit himself, in the fleshy part of his right
thigh. The force of the bullet knocked his leg out from underneath him, and he fell, which probably saved his life, as
bullets whipped through the spot where he'd been standing.

Rolling again, Gabe came up onto one knee, the rifle held
to his shoulder this time, firing as quickly as he could work
the lever. The men fired back, but, with Gabe's bullets flying
around them, they lost their concentration and began firing
wildly, without aiming.

Gabe hit each of the two men several times. The weight of
the bullets that were smashing into them drove both of them
off their feet.

Then another gun fired, a lighter sound than the sharp crack
of the rifles, and Gabe felt a crushing impact on his left side,
just below the shoulder, which spun him partway around.

Not fighting the spin, he went with it, twisting to the side, and when he was facing front again, he saw that the man he'd earlier hit in the leg had drawn his pistol. He'd hit Gabe once and was firing again, but with Gabe still moving, he missed his second shot.

Gabe shot the man twice through the body. He flopped over onto his back and lay still, apparently out of the fight for good, as were his two companions.

Gabe reached for the place where he'd been hit in the side, felt the warm stickiness of his own blood. But he had no time for the wound. Hearing a cry from further down the canyon, Gabe quickly crawled back to the edge of the hillock, dragging his wounded leg. When he reached cover he snatched up the Sharps. Down below, it was just as he had figured. Having heard the ambush sprung, the Rocking H men had ridden out into the open, and now obviously intended to rush Gabe's position while the three members of the ambush team kept him busy from the rear.

Except that the three ambushers were now dead. Gabe downed two more horses before the men below figured out that the ambush must have failed. Once again they turned and raced back for cover.

The standoff continued for another hour. Gabe took advantage of the lull to look at his wounds. The leg wound was the least serious, a clean hole all the way through the muscle. It was still fairly numb, but Gabe knew, from long experience with wounds, that it would soon grow very stiff.

The wound in his side was more serious. The bullet had gone through his chest muscle, then followed the ribs around to the back beneath his armpit. As far as he could tell, the bullet had not exited, but was still in him somewhere, lodged under his back muscles. The pain was bad and he knew that it would grow worse. Also, he had lost a fair amount of blood.

Hobbling back to his horse, Gabe pulled some old shirts out of his saddle bags and tore them up for bandages. Wadding cloth into the wounds, he got them to stop bleeding, although by the time he was finished, he felt sick and dizzy from the pain and shock.

Gabe knew that the standoff could not last. After dark they would probably send more men up that little side draw, hoping to get behind him again. Next time, slowed by his wounds, he might not hear them in time.

Using his knife, he cut a straight piece of limb from a small tree, then left it propped up on a rock, hoping that from below it would look like the barrel of his Sharps. With another piece of limb serving as a crude crutch, he hobbled away to the side, to check out the little draw, to see if there was some way he could close it off to the posse.

What he saw when he entered the draw pleased him. The three men he'd killed had ridden their mounts up the draw, then left them behind as they closed in on him over the last hundred yards. The horses were all tethered to low bushes, placidly cropping grass. Gabe untied the animals and led them back to where his own horse was tied. There was a certain amount of horse talk, some snuffling and low whickering, but no horse fights, so, after tying the other three animals near his own, Gabe crawled back to his lookout point.

He caught a glimpse of a hat behind a rock. He had no idea whether it was sitting on a man's head, or perhaps just being held up on a stick to test Gabe's alertness. Taking no chances, Gabe put a bullet through the crown, sending the hat spinning away among the rocks.

Leaving the stick pointing menacingly toward the men below, Gabe carefully backed away, until he was among the horses. He tied them all together on a long rope, his own mount included. He decided to ride one of the dead men's horses, to save his own. It was not easy getting up into the saddle, his leg was quite stiff by now, and his left arm nearly useless, but he made it, and rode off up the canyon with the horses all strung out on the lead line, hoping that his going would not be visible to the men hidden below.

He rode steadily. It grew dark, but still he pushed on, thankful there were no signs of immediate pursuit behind him. He knew that the posse would eventually discover his absence, had probably done so by now. They'd be on his trail once again, angry over the death of the three men. It was imperative that he lose them.

When it was just beginning to grow light, he came upon the situation he wanted. The trail passed through a good-sized stream, with hard, rocky ground bordering one bank further up. Stopping the horses in mid-stream, he dismounted from his borrowed horse, and climbed down onto a big rock. Dizzy and slightly feverish by now, with his wounds hurting very badly, he nearly slipped, which would have been disastrous, because, weak as he was, the slight current would have been sufficient to sweep him away from the horses.

Finally, using the lead rope to guide his own horse up to the rock, he managed to mount. He then cut the line hooking the horses together. A crack of the rope end against the haunches of the nearest horse, accompanied by a low whoop, was enough to spook the animals, and a moment later all but his own mount were splashing through the stream and running up the far bank.

As he had hoped, they split up, each going its own way. Being herd animals, they might come together again, but by then they would have done their job, churning up the bank and leaving several trails to follow.

Gabe rode his horse upstream, finally leaving the water where a shield of rock came right down into the stream bed, giving him a place where he could ride away without leaving any tracks.

For the next couple of hours he used every trick that he'd learned as a boy, all the various ways a young Lakota warrior was taught to throw off anyone who might be on his trail. By midmorning he judged that he had finally shaken his pursuers for good . . . if they were actually still after him. He'd killed a lot of their horses; they may have returned to town, or to the Rocking H ranch for fresh mounts.

Which might not do him much good if he didn't get some help soon. By now he was so weak that he was hardly able to sit in the saddle. Waves of fever swept through him, making him reel dangerously. He knew that if he fell and his horse ran off, he was a dead man.

Sitting unsteadily on his horse, Gabe looked around him, hoping to find a cave, or some other place to go to ground, but the land was mostly flat, with little cover. Then he realized that this was familiar land, land over which he had recently ridden.

In his semi-delirious state, it took him a while to make the connection. For a few seconds all he could think of was a woman, the sight of a bare breast. And then the connections began to come together, and he realized that he was not more than a mile or two from Kate's place.

But was that of any value? Would her memory of a favor done overcome her alarm when a badly wounded, nearly-dead fugitive rode into her ranch yard?

He'd have to chance it. Gabe rode that last mile, his horse nearly as tired as he was, plodding along leadenly. By the time Gabe reached the ranch, he was hallucinating badly. He never did have much of a recollection of actually riding into the ranch yard, but afterwards he thought he was pretty sure that he could remember Kate's face, and the worry in her large, startled eyes. And after that . . . nothing.

CHAPTER TWELVE

There were memories of darkness, of pain, of something cool against his skin. Once or twice he returned briefly to consciousness, each time aware of those large dark eyes before sinking back into darkness.

And then there came a time when he was able to stay conscious. No eyes this time, just a plain board ceiling above him. He was lying on a bed, in a roughly-built room. Instinctively he reached out for his weapons, only to find nothing. He muttered something in Lakota, then realized that he was not only without weapons, but he was also lying naked beneath a single blanket. He started to sit up, but felt a sharp pain catch at his left side. He gasped, and sank back down onto the bed. The rawhide thongs that made up the bedframe creaked loudly as he moved, and a moment later he heard footsteps approaching the doorway.

A moment later he was once again looking into those large dark eyes, only this time they were smiling eyes. "I think you're feeling better," Kate said.

"Better than what?" he asked, surprised by how difficult it was to talk.

"Better than the shot-to-pieces ruin who scared the hell

out of me by riding into my ranch yard and falling off his horse.''

"It was that bad?"

"Worse. For a while I thought you were going to die on me.''

Kate hesitated a moment. "Was it those men who tried to . . . . The ones you saved me from . . . were they the ones who shot you?''

"Along with some others."

Gabe saw the worry in Kate's eyes. He reassured her. "Those men. The ones who tried to hurt you. They won't try it again. They're dead."

"Good!" Kate said fiercely. Then she looked worried again. "But you said there were others."

He nodded, wincing slightly at the pain. "Uh-huh. A whole posse. I barely got away. They're probably still looking for me.''

Now Kate nodded. "I kind of figured that much. That's why I didn't send Juan for the doctor, and took the chance of patching you up myself."

Gabe reached over with his right, touched the bandages that swathed his upper body, felt the soreness of torn muscle in his right thigh. "Did you get the bullet out of my back?"

"Yes. It was fairly easy. It had stopped just beneath the skin. It was simple to cut out. The wound itself wasn't as dangerous as I'd figured at first, but you looked like you'd lost a lot of blood, and the wound was starting to go bad. I had to pour whiskey in it. Well, it was actually some kind of Mexican stuff, mescal, the last bottle that old Juan thought he was hiding from me. Then it was just a question of you staying quiet until you got some strength back."

"My . . . guns?" Gabe asked.

Now she smiled her first whole smile. "You were out of your head for a while. Yelling a lot of stuff in some other language. At least, I think it was a language. I was afraid that if you got hold of your guns you might think I was some-body else, and . . . . You know."

"Yeah. And my clothes?"

She shrugged. "I had to wash you several times. You had a fever and you were sweating up a storm."

"Thank you."

Kate laughed. "My . . . aren't we both the most polite people you ever heard of?"

He finally smiled. "It's an unusual situation."

"It doesn't seem to be. Not for you, at least. From all those scars, you seem to have a habit of getting wounded . . . bullet wounds, others that look like knife wounds. There. Look at those."

The blanket had slipped down a little, baring the upper part of Gabe's body. Kate was pointing to a series of long thin scars that seamed his upper chest and arms. "Looks like somebody tortured you. Like you got caught by some Indians."

Gabe stiffened a little, and she sensed it. "Did I say something wrong?"

He looked at her steadily for a moment. He was surprised when he finally replied; he had not intended to. Perhaps it was his physical weakness, or his gratitude for what she had done for him. "I made those scars myself."

She looked surprised, so he added. "I cut myself when my wife and my mother were killed. It's a Lakota custom . . . to cut yourself when your grief is too much to bear, when your heart can't take any more."

"Lakota?" She looked confused.

"An . . . Indian tribe. You call them the Sioux. We call ourselves the Lakota. My band was the Oglala, the Bad Faces."

She quickly scanned what she could see of him, the light skin, where it was not bronzed by the sun, the sandy hair, the light gray eyes. "You were raised by the Indians?" she asked. She'd seen half-breeds. This man was all white.

Gabe shook his head slowly. "No. I was raised by my mother."

He was aware of the confusion on Kate's face, the questions

she wanted to ask. But he was growing incredibly tired. Talking had exhausted him. While he was still trying to decide what to tell Kate, he fell asleep.

He had no idea how long he slept, but when he awoke he felt stronger. And ravenously hungry, perhaps because of the aroma of cooking meat coming from somewhere nearby. Whatever the reason, his mouth was watering by the time Kate came into the room, carrying a big bowl of what proved to be beef stew. She saw the interest in his eyes. "Can you sit up?" she asked. "Or shall I feed it to you."

"I can sit."

Sitting up was a slow process. He'd been lying too long, and his wounds had stiffened. His left side and back twinged fiercely as he tried to struggle erect. Finally, Kate helped by packing several pillows behind his back, propping him up in a fairly comfortable position.

And then it was time for the stew. He ate slowly at first, and then with more verve. The stew was delicious, and old memories returned. "Almost as good as buffalo meat," he murmured, in between mouthfuls.

"You grew up eating buffalo?" Kate asked. He stiffened a little, expecting her to start asking questions again, but although he could sense her eagerness to know more, she refrained from pushing the matter.

Perhaps it was her restraint that decided him. Or perhaps it was the position in which he found himself, wounded, his strength depleted, maybe just his gratitude toward this woman, that made him start talking. Or maybe it was also the old longing, the old memories, the chance to relive them once again.

"Yes. I grew up among the Lakota. We both lived with them, my mother and I."

He told her how his mother and father, travelling West with a wagon train back in the late forties, had heard news of possible gold in the Black Hills, and along with several others, had left the main body of the wagon train and headed further north.

"There were no white men there yet," Gabe said. "Only the Lakota and the Cheyenne. The hills were sacred ground, a place where young men went during vision quests. A place where we left our dead. It was not a healthy place for intruders."

He told her how a war party of Oglalas had surprised the gold seekers, killing all of them with the exception of his mother. "With everyone else dead, she tried to brain Little Wound—he was the leader of the band—with an empty rifle."

Gabe smiled, as if he'd been there to see it. "Little Wound was so impressed by her courage—the Lakota admire courage above all else—that he decided to spare her and take her for his woman. She was already pregnant with me. I was born among the Lakota and Little Wound became my foster father."

He did not tell Kate that at the time of the attack his mother had been pregnant with him for only a few minutes, that she and his father had made love immediately before the attack began. Nor did he tell her how for years, after he'd gotten old enough for his mother to tell him the story, he'd hated his father for putting his mother in such a dangerous predicament. How he'd despised this man he'd never known for risking everything, including his wife, because he'd become a slave of the white man's insatiable greed for gold.

"I grew up as a Lakota," Gabe said. "I was taught how to hunt as a Lakota, how to fight, how to behave as a Lakota."

"But . . . your English . . . it seems so natural to you, as if you'd grown up speaking it."

"My mother taught it to me from the time I was very young, when I was also learning Lakota. After the battle where she was taken prisoner, she managed to save her family's bible. She taught me to read from that. So I have no accent, although at times people tell me that my English is . . . different."

Kate nodded. "When I think about it, I guess it is. You . . . use words differently. Kind of formal, as if you see the world . . . ."

He smiled, and finished her statement for her. "A little as if I see the world as a cross between the Lakota way, and the way of the Old Testament. That was a strange education. One that I never wanted to end."

"But it did."

His face hardened. "Yes. When I was about fourteen. My mother knew that the white men would come soon, and that the Indian way of life would be swallowed up. I guess she spent a long time thinking about that, and about what it would mean for me. The Red Men never really understood, could never totally comprehend the power of the whites, their numbers, their technology. Being white herself, she could. She could imagine the slaughter when there were enough white men in this country, enough troops to confront the Indian. She didn't want me to be caught in that hopeless struggle, to die fighting against white soldiers. So, she finally decided that I had to go live among the whites, whether I wanted to or not, and believe me, I did not want to. I didn't want to leave The People. She arranged to have me carried off against my will, by a white man, a trapper and mountain man named Bridger."

"Jim Bridger?" Kate asked, surprised.

"Yes. You've heard of him?"

"Of course. Who hasn't."

"I hated him for taking me away from The People. Hated my mother too, because it was her idea. Later, when I was older, I was better able to understand why she did it. And then I forgave her, but way too late. Bridger . . . he came to mean a lot to me later, too. I even took his name. They used to call him Old Gabe. I became Young Gabe. But as I said, I hated him then. He took me to an army fort. They kept me there a long time, made me work like a slave. One day an army captain tried to kill me. I fought back, I hurt him, even though I was only a boy. So they put me in jail. Three years of jail. For three years I did not see the sky nor smell the earth. Then one day Bridger came and got me out. Got me back my freedom just before the beginning of Red Cloud's War, one of the few wars against the whites that the Red Man ever won. I went back to the Lakota, The People. I married a girl, an Oglala. Her name was Yellow Buckskin Girl.''

Gabe drifted off into thought for a few seconds, remembering his wife, Yellow Buckskin Girl, remembering the look and feel and smell of her. How he'd saved her from mutilation by her jealous husband, how he'd killed the man. He chose not to tell this to Kate.

''We were not together for very long,'' he said. His face was expressionless as he continued, a cold emptiness that frightened Kate. ''The soldiers attacked the camp where we were staying, attacked at dawn. They killed many people, including many women and children, my mother and my wife among them. My stepfather died too. That's when I made these cuts.''

He pointed to the scars on his chest and arms. He did not choose to tell Kate that his stepfather had been so distraught, so crazed by the death of all those that he had loved, that the sight of Gabe's white skin had caused the old man to attack Gabe, his stepson. Gabe had had to kill Little Wound in self-defense. Kill the man who'd raised him, the man he'd loved as a father.

Nor did he tell Kate that the man who'd killed both his mother and his wife had been the same army captain who'd gotten him thrown into jail. A man whom he had eventually hunted down and killed.

''Is that when you stopped living with the Indians?'' Kate asked.

Yes and no, Gabe thought. He'd left to hunt the man who'd killed those he loved. He partially evaded the question. ''I had a grandfather living in Boston,'' he said. 'My mother's father. I went to him. He helped me begin to really understand the white man's ways. He made it possible for me to move among the whites.''

Although my heart will always be Lakota, he added silently.

"I . . . found an old bible among your things," Kate said hesitantly. "It had writing around all the margins. Very small writing. I didn't read it because I thought it might be private."

"It is," Gabe said curtly. He saw the hurt on Kate's face, but there was nothing he could do about that. The bible and its writing was . . . special. During the long years she'd lived among the Lakota, his mother had managed to hang onto the white part of her identity by keeping a diary of her new life, writing it down in tiny handwriting on the only paper she had . . . the margins of her family bible. Gabe had read that diary a hundred times. He did not let others read it, had shown it only to his grandfather in Boston, who Gabe felt had a right to see what his daughter had written, how she had lived and died.

Kate had the grace not to persist. She brought the subject back to the Lakota. "You sound as if you miss your life with the Indians. Most white men would consider it very unlucky, a terrible tragedy that your mother was captured and forced to spend her life among Indians. But of course you may see it differently, you were born among them, so . . . ."

Gabe's face shone. "Yes, I was. I was a Lakota until I was almost a man, that was all I knew. That, and my mother's tales of the white world. But those tales were only a fable to me, something unreal. I lived in the real world, in the world itself, on the earth, under the sky, with everything in harmony around me, the ancient harmony between The People, the animals, the plant world, even our enemies were part of that harmony."

"Enemies?"

"Oh, yes. The Pawnee, sometimes other bands of Lakota, but most of all, the Crow. They were our traditional enemies, because a long time ago we had driven them from their ancestral lands and made those lands our own. They never forgave the Lakota."

"I've heard that Indians fight all the time. That they live in constant fear."

"Fear? Yes, there was some of that. But mostly, we just lived, we were so alive, life was so . . . immediate. We lived right then, in the moment, wherever we were at that moment. We didn't live in the future like the white man, we were content with each separate instant, even if it sometimes brought us sorrows. The world was all around us, alive, unending. Each hour, moment, day, was so real. And above all, we had ourselves, The People. We were all as one, a family, who, although we might fight among ourselves from time to time, were one thing. I don't think I could ever explain to a white man, who grew up as a white man, what that meant to us. Our oneness. I don't mean that we all did exactly the same things, that we had no independence. Each man was free, free to do as he wanted, moment by moment. But we were still one."

"I gather that the women were not very free," Kate said, somewhat acerbically.

Gabe smiled. "Only a little. But they were one with the rest of us, too. It's a life I miss. I feel empty in the white man's world, where each person is separated, not only from one another but from the world around them, the magical world, the Lakota world."

He waited a moment before continuing. "But there is no going back. That world, the old world, has been destroyed forever. There is no world left but the white man's world. And I am in it . . . even if I am not part of it."

CHAPTER THIRTEEN

Gabe and Kate became lovers almost by accident, although perhaps it was inevitable. Gabe's natural strength and health, aided by a lifetime living out of doors, made his wounds mend quickly. But because he was still confined to bed, his torn and wounded muscles began to stiffen. To speed the healing process, Kate began to give Gabe massages. Of course, as she massaged, she could not fail to admire her patient's lean, hard body. Nor could Gabe fail to be aware of his nurse's abundant femininity.

One day, after Kate had worked for a while on Gabe's chest and shoulder muscles, it was time to pay attention to his wounded right leg. While working on his chest, she had, quite naturally, been bending over him, and the low-necked Mexican-style blouse that Juan's wife had made for her tended to fall away from her breasts, giving Gabe a close view of Kate's impressive cleavage. At times her breasts were only a few inches from his face, so, when Kate finally abandoned his chest and moved lower on the bed to work on his leg, it was not strange at all that Gabe was by then showing some rather natural effects of Kate's overpowering proximity.

The main effect was quite noticeable. It was a warm day,

and Gabe was covered only by a sheet. The sheet had been pulled down to his waist so that Kate could work on his chest. Now she began to pull it up his right leg, only to notice that the sheet had tented into a high peak . . . right above his groin.

Kate froze, with her hands held rather clumsily in front of her a few inches away from Gabe's right thigh. Her eyes remained riveted on that tented sheet. She suddenly found it difficult to breathe. Guiltily, her eyes flicked up toward Gabe's. "Sorry about that," he said, although he didn't look sorry at all.

"I . . . don't be," she murmured back. "It's . . . only natural. Just . . . natural."

And the more she thought about nature and its wonderful ways, the more she began to realize that her own body was in the midst of a rather natural reaction to the close and intimate proximity of Gabe's undoubtedly masculine body; a melting wetness suffused the area between her thighs.

"Just natural," they both murmured, almost together, and now their eyes had locked, full of inevitability, glittering hotly.

Kate had no memory of taking off her clothes, but somehow they disappeared. Then the sheet ended up on the floor, baring Gabe's erection, to Kate's eyes a most monumental phenomenon, riveting, compelling, irresistibly inviting.

Since Gabe still did not have the full use of his left arm and shoulder, Kate did most of the work, straddling his lower body, guiding him into her. "It's so long . . . so long," she whimpered as she settled down onto him. Gabe wondered if she was complimenting him, but then she added, "So long a time . . . it's been such an incredibly long time," and he knew that she had been referring to her enforced lack of a man.

Which she was quickly making up for, plunging and rearing and whimpering above him, with her big round breasts jiggling and bouncing almost in his face, forcing Gabe to rethink his opinion of white women, at least of this white woman.

Their first coupling was over very quickly, ending in a wild mutual explosion. Over the next few days there were repeat performances, a pleasant light exercise, the nature of which seemed to help Gabe heal even more quickly.

After each episode of lovemaking they planned and plotted, and the focus of their plans revolved around Colonel Harlan Harrison, their joint nemesis. "He killed my husband," Kate said bitterly. "He's trying to steal my ranch, and if I won't let him, then he'll try to kill me too. I want that bastard's hide."

Gabe wanted it too, partly because of the bullets that Harrison had indirectly put into his body, partly for what Harrison had done to The People, because he was now convinced that Harrison must have had a hand, and probably a leading hand, in the theft of the cattle that should have been sent to the reservation.

However, revenge was not enough. In addition, Gabe hoped to ensure an adequate future supply of beef for the reservation's inhabitants. That would take a lot more planning and strategy than simple revenge.

But Gabe's freedom of movement was restricted. One day, after a trip to town to buy supplies, old Juan reported that the hue and cry over Gabe was still as strong as ever. "They want him for killing all those Harrison men," Juan said gleefully. Then he grew more serious. "I think that if they catch him, there will be a very quick hanging."

So Gabe would need help. He already knew where he could ask for that help. By then he was out of bed and moving around. He still limped, and his left arm was stiff and somewhat weak, but he knew that exercise and activity would soon remedy both those situations.

The first step in his plans was to ask Kate to do something for him in town; he obviously couldn't go there himself, so one morning Kate had Juan help her harness a couple of horses to the buckboard, then set out on the two hour drive into town.

As she travelled, she was filled with an eager joy, partly based on the prospect of finally settling the score with her mortal enemy, partly because of the pleasure Gabe had brought to her body. Despite the rigid joylessness that the malign influence of poor, sad, frozen old Queen Victoria had laid over the Western world like a curse, Kate was a highly physical young woman, and not even a little bit ashamed of it. Gabe had made her body feel wonderful, made her mind alive again, and given her hope. And today would see the first of the many nails that she would help drive, one by one, into Harlan Harrison's long overdue coffin.

Once in town, Kate made a few stops to purchase supplies, and buy herself some new clothes. Since her husband's death money had been tight, but Gabe had insisted that she take fifty dollars from him. She had huffily refused; she was a proud woman, but he'd insisted. "You've got to cover the real reason for your trip," he insisted. "And the best way to do that is to spend money on woman things."

So it was in between shopping stops—which she had to admit she enjoyed very much—that she finally took care of her real mission—a quick and clandestine visit to the telegraph office.

Then . . . potential disaster. She was on her way back toward the general store when she ran into Harrison. Or nearly ran into him, because he was standing right in the middle of the boardwalk, blocking her way. "Why . . . mornin', Kate," he said unctuously. "Haven't seen you in town for one hell of a long time."

"My name is Miller," she said, doing her best to keep her voice level. "Mrs. Miller."

A slight sneer tugged at Harrison's lips, as if to taunt her with: "Then where is Mr. Miller?" and she knew with a total certainty that she wanted to see this man dead. For a moment she experienced a moment's fear that he might have seen her come out of the telegraph office. If he had, it would not take much pressure from a man of Harrison's local importance to force from the operator the nature of the message she had sent.

But Harrison had been coming from the opposite direction, and there seemed to be no indication of suspicion on his face, only arrogance and a kind of half-suppressed gloating.

'Colonel' Harlan Harrison was a big man, and technically, he was not bad-looking. He dressed fairly well for this part of the world, wearing today, as usual, a dark coat, a string tie, expensive trousers, and fancy, hand-made boots. His hair was dark and well-cut, and only lightly flecked with grey. He wore a short, neatly-cut beard.

But there were subtle flaws that marred the total picture. His expression was saved from weakness only by the intensity of the greed that fired his every action. His eyes, while cruel and hard, did not quite meet one's gaze, and he had little nervous mannerisms that betrayed an inner insecurity . . . once again bolstered by the ever-present greed. Add to the total picture Harrison's Texas whine, and you had a man Kate would have found easy to despise even if he had never harmed her and hers.

"Please stand aside," she said coldly. "I want to pass. Preferably upwind."

Anger flared in his eyes, and for a moment Kate wondered if she had gone too far, if perhaps he would strike her right here in the middle of the boardwalk. But Harrison chose to exercise that marvelous old Southern gallantry, the kind that had always been so effective in keeping Southern womanhood suitably subservient. "Ya'll should be careful of annoyin' your true friends, Kate. Insult me enough, an' I may be forced to withdraw my offer to buy your ranch. An' a rat gen'rous offer it is."

"Before I'd sell to you," Kate replied, barely able to keep the intensity of her anger from making her voice shake, "I'd burn down the buildings, shoot my cattle, and pour salt on the soil."

She swept past him, and, afraid that she might somehow

give herself away, decided to forget about the visit she'd planned to the milliners', for a new dress, and instead, after buying a few more supplies, she had the store owners pile what she had already bought into the back of the buckboard, and then set out for home.

But as she covered the miles, she was uncomfortable. As the full force of her final words had sunk into Harrison, she had been aware of the hot gleam of hatred and anger in his eyes, and she would not put it past him to surprise her out here on the trail. Or to send some of his men out to do what he wouldn't want to be caught doing personally. Rough as this country was, harassing or harming a woman, particularly a decent widow woman, was one sure way of gaining the enmity of the entire population, good man and bad alike. So far that had been Kate's main protection . . . until Harrison had sent those three pigs out to the ranch to teach her a lesson.

She ground her teeth as she remembered what they had been ready to do to her. Then felt a surge of elation when she remembered that they were now dead. And that they had been killed by the man who was now her lover. Her strong, deadly lover.

Kate was no shrinking violet. She was the hard, remorseless product of a hard and remorseless land. And as she rode closer and closer to home, to her land, the land she was willing to defend with her life, she moved her shotgun closer to where she sat, and dreamed hot dreams of the man who had come into her life, mixed with dreams of the most bloody revenge imaginable.

CHAPTER FOURTEEN

Ten days later, Kate's telegram bore fruit. Early one afternoon an apparition rode into the ranch yard, a young man mounted on a tall bay horse, dress in, what were by local standards, bizarre clothing; a suit of the latest cut in a bright houndstooth pattern, and beneath the suit jacket, a brightly striped silk vest, green silk shirt, and the largest and floppiest foulard tie that Kate had ever seen. A black derby hat, perhaps a trifle too small, rode high on the man's head. Instead of boots he wore, partly covered by gray silk spats, narrow shoes with tapering heels. The Big City had come to the Black Hills.

Juan kept an old dog of uncertain parentage. It began to yap the moment the stranger rode into the yard, and kept dashing back and forth near the legs of the stranger's horse.

Juan poked his head out of the house he shared with his wife and children, took one look at the stranger, then ducked back inside, as if the splendor of the sight had hurt his eyes.

Kate walked out onto the porch and stood looking at the stranger, wondering what he was selling. She noticed that Juan was now standing in the doorway of his house, holding his antique muzzle-loading shotgun. The stranger noticed it too, but he nevertheless turned away from Juan and smiled down at Kate. "Are you Kate Miller?" he asked, in the harsh accent of the New York streets.

"Why . . . yes, I am."

"Then let me introduce myself, ma'am. Rory Cavanaugh, answering your telegram."

By now, Gabe, having heard the commotion, and having recognized the rider from his vantage point behind the window drapes, now came out onto the porch, walking with the aid of a stick—his right leg was still a little weak. "Rory!" he called out. "What kept you? Meet a lady along the trail?"

Rory shook his head. "Uh-uh. It was the trail itself. The railroad ended a million miles from here, and it's been the hinges of hell ever since."

He brushed at the lapels of his suit, which was loaded down with considerable dust. "Why you always end up in the middle of nowhere, I'll never know. Why, just once, couldn't we meet in a civilized place?"

Gabe raised his eyebrows. "Like New York? Or would that be stretching the meaning of the word civilized just a little too far?"

Rory grinned and swung down from his horse. Kate noticed that he did it with the grace and ease of a man in fine physical condition. She also noticed that, underneath the garish clothing, this Rory Cavanaugh was quite good-looking, with thick black hair and intriguing green eyes. Irish stock, she thought, Black Irish.

The quick glance that Rory threw her way travelled all the way up and down her body, and she saw admiration in his eyes. Which pleased her mightily. This man was full of that old Celtic magic.

Then all his attention was on Gabe, and all of Gabe's on Rory. Kate instinctively realized that there was a powerful bond between these two men, and she experienced an uncharacteristic twinge of jealousy. Don't be a fool, she warned herself.

Gabe led Rory into the house, right over to the fireplace.

There had been a little snap in the air earlier in the morning; autumn was approaching, and the remnants of the morning's fire still glowed on the hearth. Gabe hobbled over to the scuttle to get some wood, and soon had a blaze going, although obviously not because of the fire's warmth; it was a hot day. No, there was something ceremonial in the way he laid the fire, got it going again, then sat Rory down on the big buffalo robe in front of the fireplace.

That was odd, too, the men choosing to sit on a rug, on the floor, instead of using chairs. Rory looked slightly uncomfortable as he settled down cross-legged, with the heels of his shoes digging into his thighs. But Kate noticed that he made no mention of chairs.

Before sitting down himself, Gabe went over to his saddle-bags and rummaged around inside for a moment, finally extracting a long narrow object about a foot and a half long, wrapped in what looked like doeskin.

He took the bundle over to the buffalo rug, where he sat near Rory, sinking down easily, as if he'd lived on the floor most of his life, which, Kate realized, he undoubtedly had.

She watched him unwrap the bundle. Inside was a long Indian pipe, the kind she and other whites thought of as a peace pipe, along with a small bundle of some weird-looking stuff that was probably tobacco.

Gabe began another process—loading the pipe. Once again, it seemed to have ceremonial overtones. Then he looked up and saw Kate watching him. He didn't exactly frown, but she could tell that her presence made him uncomfortable. Hey, mister, she thought angrily. I'm not one of your obedient little Indian women. I don't disappear into the woodwork like a good little girl whenever the men feel like talking.

But there was something in those pale gray eyes, not exactly anger, or the promise of danger, but rather a slight disappointment, which made Kate decide to swallow her pride and, if not leave the room, at least move to the other side, near the cookstove, where she pretended to busy herself with this and that.

Gabe felt relief. Caught between cultures for a moment, he had felt ill at ease. The intrusion of a woman into the activities of the next few minutes would interfere with the right feeling, and the right feeling was what he intended to establish. So far, from the first day he'd ridden into Harrison's town, he'd been involved in action after action, without recharging himself, without returning to the source of all power. Now, with Rory here, it was time to renew his strength, to call out to the invisible world.

The fire in the fireplace was important; fire brought men's minds into harmony, and he and Rory had a lot to talk about; they'd need harmony. Smoking the pipe together would then connect the both of them with . . . with that which could not be directly talked about.

The pipe's bowl was made from a soft red stone that was found only in Minnesota; the Oglala had always traded with the Minnesota Lakota tribes for pipe stone. The stem was made of a piece of hollow willow bark. Four pieces of colored cloth hung from the pipe stem, along with an eagle feather. The four strips of cloth represented the four directions, from which all things came. The eagle feather represented *Wakan Tanka*, the Great Spirit, that which was above all else. Gabe treasured this particular pipe. It had been given to him by the old Oglala warrior and seer, Two Face, just before the army had hung him. It had remained with Gabe ever since.

He tamped the bowl full of *chanshasha*, a mixture of wild tobacco and willow bark. Then, holding the bowl in his left hand, the stem in his right, he ceremoniously presented the pipe to the four directions, West, North, East, and South, then held it down toward the earth, and finally, up toward the sky. Only then did he scoop a coal from the fire and place it inside the pipe's bowl, lighting the tobacco. He raised the pipe to his lips and drew in some of the pungent smoke, and as it went into him he felt power entering his body along with the smoke. How good it felt, to do this thing which joined a man to all that there was.

He passed the pipe to Rory, who smoked too, although he coughed a little at the strength of the tobacco. Smoking the pipe did not mean the same to Rory that it meant to Gabe. Rory always went along with it anyhow, because he knew how important this little ritual was to his friend.

Gabe watched as Rory smoked. Strange, how their lives had come together. Years before, after leaving the white man's jail and returning to the Oglala, after the death of his mother and of his wife, Gabe, then called Long Rider, his Oglala name, had taken part with other Oglalas in the derailing of a train. All of the train's passengers had been slaughtered— with the exception of a fifteen year old boy, Rory, who'd stood over the bodies of his mother and father, calmly trying to reload an empty pistol as Oglala warriors closed in around him.

Long Rider had been as impressed by the boy's courage as the other warriors. But Long Rider felt something more. He remembered himself, at more or less the same age, stranded among enemies, the whites, thrown into their foul jail, cut off from those he loved.

On impulse, he'd saved the boy, much to the anger of the other warriors. They would have enjoyed the prestige of killing one so brave, of taking his scalp, but a warrior of Long Rider's prestige was not a man one casually affronted, and since it had been his knowledge of the white man's ways that had permitted them to derail the train, they let him keep the boy, whom Gabe protected, showing him how to survive in the wilderness.

Later, when Long Rider returned to the white man's world to hunt down the man who'd killed his mother and his wife, it was Rory who'd showed him how to live among the whites, how to dress, where to buy the things he needed, how to blend in. And it was Rory who'd eventually helped him kill his enemy. As Kate had sensed, there was a very strong bond between the two of them.

Over the next hour Gabe explained the situation to Rory, as much of it as he understood. ''So I think we need a man in town,'' Gabe concluded. ''Someone not publicly connected to me, someone who would hopefully be able to find out more about the connection between Peebles and Harrison. To work from within.''

Gabe grinned, then added, ''And maybe scatter around a little fear and havoc.''

Rory grinned too. ''Yep. Sounds like it. Sounds like it could be one hell of a lot of fun.''

Gabe's grin continued. ''Of course. Why else would I call you out of that cesspool you call a city?''

From across the room, Kate winced. Oh, God, men. They were going to fight dangerous antagonists, probably kill people, and they were talking about the whole situation as if it was just for the sport of it. Well, maybe in Gabe's case it was for something more, considering his attachment to those people out on the reservation. Not that she should complain . . . if Gabe and Rory permanently took care of that son of a bitch, Harrison.

But she wasn't in it for the fun. Just for the revenge.

CHAPTER FIFTEEN

Rory rode into town the next day. He made a grand entrance, as he had intended, since his plan was to attract as much attention as possible. His big city clothing helped, as did the large tip he gave the semislave who carried his gear up to his hotel room.

Choosing a hotel had been no great problem; the town had only one, a two story affair of warped pine planking, but the hotel's builders, perhaps having expected the town to grow more than it eventually did, had made efforts at grandeur; velveteen wallpaper in the hallways, water spotted now, boot-scarred carpeting, and, most ambitious of all, a small chandelier in the dining room, which had somehow managed to remain unbroken.

Rory insisted on second floor accommodations; it was more difficult for potential enemies to come in through upper floor windows. The room itself was pleasingly large, which he expected for sixty cents a day. True, the bed springs did sag a little, as did one corner of the floor, but one of the room's two windows overlooked the main street, while the other gave him a rather limited view of an alley below. A possible back way out, if he didn't mind the drop.

Although the commode's marble top was slightly cracked, Rory decided that it was genuine marble. The commode held a rather nice pitcher and basin, the pitcher containing relatively clean water, and after his bags had been deposited and the man who'd carried them into the room staggered off, dazed, holding a fifty cent piece in one grimy paw, Rory took off his coat, tie, and shirt, and spent a few minutes washing up.

Next he dug into the big gladstone that was his main item of luggage—other than his Winchester—and got out a clean shirt and tie. Digging a little deeper, he retrieved his shoulder rig. Unlike Gabe, he wore the holster underneath his left arm, and kept it filled with a Smith and Wesson .32 caliber double action revolver. Gabe had initially ridiculed the little pistol . . . until the day Rory used it to drop a man who was about to put a bullet into the back of Gabe's head. One of the nicest things about the little .32 was that it was so concealable; when he put on his coat there was next to no bulge at all, and to a clothes horse like Rory, that was important.

Judging that he was now suitably attired, Rory went downstairs. The hotel boasted few luxuries, but it did have a dining room—which Rory regretted patronizing after he'd grimly tried to plow his way through one of the toughest steaks and some of the greasiest fried potatoes he'd ever encountered.

Pushing his half-full plate away, Rory signaled to the waiter—who was also the desk clerk. The waiter came over cautiously. Ever since he'd started working in the dining room he'd received all kinds of reactions over the food, some of them quite violent. Imagine his wonder, then, when Rory not only smiled, but also pushed a quarter toward him in what could only be intended as a tip. "Tell me, my good man," Rory said, still smiling. "Would there be a possibility of finding a game of chance in your fair town?"

The waiter looked puzzled. Rory wondered if it was the incredible overstatement of calling this burg "fair," of calling it anything else but the miserable frontier hole it was. "A card game," he prompted. "Poker, faro . . . ."

The man's eyes showed their first glimmering of possible intelligence. "Oh, yeah . . . sure. Over to the saloon."

Then his face showed concern. This, after all, was a paying customer, one who left *tips*, a man to be cherished above all other men. "Kind of a rough place," he warned. "Them gents over there take their card-playin' real serious-like."

Rory's smile grew even broader. "So do I, my man. So do I."

Rory sauntered on over to the saloon, his stomach rumbling. He'd have to do something about finding food fit to eat. Had to keep up his strength. Maybe he'd locate that rooming house Gabe had told him about, get the old girl who ran it to feed him. Not that he'd stay there. Not public enough.

The saloon was not difficult to find, an unconscious drunk laying in the street right in front of its swinging double doors. A piano tinkled tinnily from inside, and besides, Rory could smell it, smell the odor of unwashed bodies, cheap whiskey, spilled beer. To Rory, the stench was transmogrified into the sweet odor of potential profit, because when the unwashed and ignorant came into contact with strong spirits, what pitiful amounts of money they had somehow managed to amass inevitably drained away . . . hopefully into Rory Cavanaugh's pockets.

As he went in through the swinging doors, Rory almost gave too much of himself away. The instant he was inside, knowing that he was still silhouetted against the outdoor light, he instinctively moved to one side, along the wall, a trick that Gabe had taught him some time ago, after Rory's city carelessness had almost gotten them both killed.

He glanced around quickly. Apparently no one had noticed his little move. Good. He wanted to build, in this town, not the reputation of a careful gunfighter, but rather the reputation of a hail-fellow-well-met, a man anyone could trust.

However, as he stepped deeper into the room, he noticed some dark spots on the warped wooden flooring. Old blood stains, not quite soaked up by the dirty sawdust. No doubt from the fight Gabe had told him about.

To Rory's satisfaction, a card game was in progress. Three men were grouped around a table halfway back in the room. Rory walked to the bar and ordered a glass of whiskey, hoping the whiskey's antiseptic properties would cancel out the dirty glass, then wandered over toward the card game.

Two dusty cowhands were playing five card stud against a small ferrety man dressed in a rather tattered suit. It was obviously the cowhands against the ferrety man. They seemed to be friends, and were cheering one another on each time one of them bet against the man in the suit. From the way the man in the suit was flipping the cards around, Rory figured that he was a professional gambler. Rory also decided, after watching a few hands, that he was not a very good professional gambler. Small town stuff. Not that a gambler would have to be very good to survive against these two cowboy amateurs; the ferrety man already had a small pile of their money stacked up in front of him.

Rory had been standing a few feet away, leaning against the bar, sipping his drink, careful to sip very little of it. Now he walked up to the table. "Got room for another player?" he asked amiably.

He got differing reactions. The two cowhands, looking up, rather startled by this stranger's magnificence, immediately smelled dude, and a chance to repair their fortunes. The gambler, on the other hand, immediately looked suspicious, but it was too late. "Shore, stranger, set on down," said one of the cowhands. "That is, if'n yew kin afford the tariff. We're playin' a two cent ante, with a quarter limit."

Rory pulled out a chair, and before sitting down, rummaged in an inner pocket and pulled out a handful of money, some of it small change, but the rest in gold—including several twenty dollar double eagles. The cowhands' eyes gleamed, and even the little gambler, who should have known better, let his avarice get the upper hand over his usual caution.

They had to call the bartender over to provide Rory with change. Rory insisted that the bartender also bring a bottle of whiskey, which Rory put right in the middle of the table, indicating with a munificent wave of his hand that his playing partners were to feel free to drink all of it they wished. He noticed that there were no demands from the other men that he let them pay their share. Obviously a bunch of two-bit small-timers.

The game went smoothly. Rory made sure it did, he was a master poker player, and had used the game for years to provide himself with pocket money. It was as if the existence of the game were a magic, bottomless treasure chest from which he could extract a basic living any time he needed funds.

Of course, when playing with the type of players he now had against him, Rory was always careful never to win too much, never to scare them off. As this particular game progressed he even let the two cowhands get ahead of him from time to time, although never too far ahead. It was important to make them think that they had a chance. If he cleaned them out quickly, if he took the last of their money, if he made a big show of winning, then other men, chastened by the example, might decide not to play against him at all.

No, he took only part of their money, starting first with the ferrety little gambler, slowly redistributing the man's winnings, making sure that the cowhands got their fair share. When the gambler was down a few dollars from his original stake, he looked Rory straight in the eye, gave him a little nod that indicated he knew a master player when he saw one, then withdrew from the game.

Other men began to grow interested. They noticed all that loose cash stacked in front of Rory, saw the clumsy way he sometimes seemed to play. They also saw the smiles on the faces of the two cowhands, who, having gotten some of their losings back from the ferrety card shark, didn't realize that, overall, they were losing. Nor that Rory was steadily pulling ahead. He had a knack for unobtrusively slipping small portions of his winnings back into his pockets, so that the pile of money in front of him did not seem to grow.

Within an hour there were a dozen men sitting around the table, hunched over their cards. Rory saw to it that the original two cowhands left with modest winnings, making sure, of course, that the money did not come out of his own stake. Now they would tell others about the dude who was such an easy touch in a card game.

Rory played for several hours, using every trick he knew to keep his opponents happy. Eventually his concentration began to lag, and he was considering a graceful retreat from the table when he heard someone call out a name that caught his attention. "What'll you have tonight, Mr. Peebles," the bartender was saying.

"I'll start with a beer, Joe."

Rory turned casually, and saw a slightly-built, balding, nondescript man standing at the bar. This must be the Indian agent Gabe had told him about. He certainly fit the description, right down to the weakness written across his face.

Over the next half-hour Rory covertly watched Peebles, diverting enough of his attention so that he actually lost a hand or two that he had not intended to lose. At the end of that half hour, Rory, who was, like all good poker players, a good judge of character, had pegged Peebles as not only a weak, but also a lonely man. He could read the loneliness in the rather diffident way Peebles glanced around the room, in the way that he seemed to be apart from what was going on.

Rory might have felt sorry for Peebles . . . if he had not already known that this was a man who had tried to get his partner killed, a man who had not even had the guts to do the dirty work himself. And he also knew that Peebles was a thief, the worst kind of thief . . . a man who stole food from people who were starving.

CHAPTER SIXTEEN

Rory decided to stay in the saloon a while longer. As he continued playing cards, he covertly eyed Peebles, noticing that, while the man had started with a beer, drinking rather slowly, the drinking got faster. He drank two more beers, then Peebles switched to whiskey. Peebles was clearly a drinker.

Rory finally got up to leave. There were mutters from some of the other players, the more stupid ones, who hated to see such an easy mark slip out of their grasp. Rory was all smiles as he left the table. On his way past Peebles he nodded pleasantly. Peebles looked slightly surprised, then rather hesitantly nodded back.

Over the next few days Rory kept it at that level, just a nod and a smile at Peebles whenever he saw him. But he made no attempt to talk to him, to draw him into a premature conversation. In the meantime, he continued playing cards in the saloon, making himself a local fixture, a man others would recognize as a regular, someone to accept.

There was one deviation in his plan, one that Rory was afraid would mark him as someone to be avoided. He was playing a little more seriously one day; a couple of his opponents were men from out of town, and damned good card players. Despite the increased competition, Rory managed to pull way ahead, which annoyed one of the strangers. "You get too damned many good cards, friend," he said sullenly, while watching Rory rake in a good-sized pot. "Especially when you're dealin'."

Rory looked up sharply, staring the other man straight in the eye. The other man tried to stare straight back, but something in Rory's eyes stopped him, and he looked away.

But that was not the end of it. Two hands later Rory won big again, most of the money coming from the mouthy stranger. The stranger had been drinking. Now he put down another good-sized belt of bar whiskey, then said, fairly loudly, "God, but I hate a cheat."

Rory looked up, once again locking eyes with the stranger, and this time the stranger did not look away; the whiskey had added iron to his spine. "Would you be talking about anyone at this table?" Rory asked quietly.

He could have let it pass, he doubted that the man would have pressed the point. But Rory also knew that several other men had heard the stranger's words, and the kiss of death in this, or in any saloon where card players convened, would be to let anyone call him a card cheat and not do something about it. Others might then become convinced that he did cheat, which would ruin him in this town.

The stranger was a big man, somewhat blubbery, but with broad sloping shoulders that promised great strength. He probably outweighed Rory by fifty or sixty pounds. The stranger hesitated, but only for a moment. Perhaps the gentleness of Rory's voice had given him further courage. "I'm talking about you, shitface," he said more confidently. "No man wins as many hands in a row as you have, without a little fancy card work. I'll bet you got some surprises up those fancy sleeves, like maybe an ace or two. I think I'll take a look."

Fortunately, the man was as stupid as he was big. He reached across the table with his right hand to pluck at Rory's left sleeve. The table was wide enough to make him stretch, and when Rory judged that the other man was sufficiently off balance he simply seized his opponent's right wrist with his own left, and pulled him toward him. The man lurched forward, and when his head was close enough, Rory half-rose and slammed the heel of his right hand into the side of the other man's face.

The man slumped down onto the table top, scattering cards and money. Rory hoped it would end there, but he doubted it; the stranger had just lost a great deal of face in front of a roomful of people. He'd want to even the score.

Rory glanced at the man's companion, but his hands were clearly in sight on top of the table, and his face was blank. He looked away from Rory's gaze. Apparently he intended to stay out of it.

The man Rory had hit shook his head dizzily. Then he spotted Rory, who was now on his feet, standing well clear of the table. The stranger roared out an oath, and surged to his feet too, knocking the table half over. "That was a sucker punch!" he bellowed, starting toward Rory, his huge arms reaching out for Rory's throat.

"You should know," Rory replied without heat. He simply brushed the man's hands out of the way, then stepped in close, hammering the top of his head against an unprotected face. Blood gushed from the other man's nose, tears of pain blinded him, and while he was clawing at his face, Rory stepped in even closer, and kneed the man in the groin.

"Waauufff!" the man grunted, forgetting his broken nose for the moment. He bent over forward, both hands diving down between his legs in a vain effort to press away the agonizing pain. Rory grabbed the man's hair in both hands and pulled his head down toward his knee, which was rising rapidly.

Everyone in the bar could hear the man's teeth crash together as Rory's knee slammed into his chin. The man stood for a moment, bent over, eyes blank, and then started to fall. Rory helped him fall a little faster by slamming his right fist against the back of the man's neck. The rickety wooden building shook as the man hit the floor, where he lay without moving, his breath snoring loudly in his throat.

Although his opponent was down and out, Rory did not yet relax. Alert, muscles ready, his eyes scanned the room. He had learned long ago that one of the most dangerous times in a fight was when you had just put down one man, and got too confident, and then somebody else sandbagged you from behind.

But this time the men closest to him were backing away, and no one looked hostile. Indeed, most looked admiring. "There's one damned good alley fighter," one man murmured to another.

The fallen man's companion got slowly to his feet. He went over to where he lay, looking down sorrowfully. "Old Pete just can't hold his likker," he said in a matter-of-fact way. "Someday he's gonna get hisself killed."

A couple of other men helped him drag Pete over toward the door. By the time they got him there, Pete was coming to. His friend helped him to his feet. Pete almost fell again, but his friend looped Pete's arm around his shoulders. Pete looked around blearily. "Wha . . . What hit me?" he mumbled.

"Got kicked by a horse," the friend said patiently. "Come on . . . time we got back to our room."

Rory watched them leave, keeping the doorway in sight until he was certain that they were gone. More than once he'd had a beaten foe come charging back into the room with a gun in his hand and murder in his eyes.

He finally sat back down at the table. He hadn't noticed it before but Peebles was standing at the bar. Rory wondered if he'd been there long enough to see the fight. Probably so, because as Peebles looked at him—the first time he'd looked straight at Rory without looking away—he seemed impressed.

Rory smiled at Peebles, nodded. Peebles nodded back.

Rory was tempted to make his move then, but held back, judging that the time was not quite right.

The next day the right time finally arrived. It was late afternoon, the sun was sinking low in the west. Rory was walking along the boardwalk in front of Peebles's office . . . just as Peebles was coming out. The two men nearly ran into one another. Rory nodded amicably to Peebles, then glanced at the sign over the office door. "I didn't know that you were the Indian agent."

Peebles nodded. Rory thought he saw a slight gleam of suspicion in the other man's eyes. Probably from a guilty conscience, Rory figured, but aloud he said, "It's an undervalued job, Indian agent. I admire a man who has the sand to do that kind of work."

Peebles blinked, and now there was a slight glow of pleasure on his face. "Why do you say that?" he asked, the first words he'd ever spoken to Rory.

"Hell, man. It's a critical job. If there was no one to do it, who'd keep those scalping savages off our backs? Who'd keep our women and kids safe?"

"I think you're confusing me with the army," Peebles protested. But there was no missing the pleasure in his voice, which was what Rory had been angling for, which had guided him in his choice of words, the implication that there was danger from the scattered remnants of a beaten people, giving Peebles a chance to rationalize his own treachery in stealing from them. Peebles smiled at Rory. "I'm pleased to meet a man who recognizes even a little of what the job entails."

"Hell, man, everyone should. Say . . . where are you heading?"

"Why . . . home."

Rory shrugged, a little theatrically. "You can let home wait until later. There should be a game starting up over at the saloon. Why don't you and I wander over that way? I'd be honored as hell to play cards with you. My name's Rory. Rory Cavanaugh."

Out of habit, Peebles hesitated. Then he smiled again.

"Why not?" he asked. "Why not have a little fun? I'm John Peebles."

There were only two men playing poker when Rory and Peebles entered the saloon. Good, safe, mediocre players. He and Peebles sat in, and all during the game Rory remained as jovial as possible, spending attention on Peebles without seeming to overdo it. It took little coaching to get Peebles to put down a healthy ration of whiskey. And he made sure that Peebles won, he even sacrificed a good deal of his own money. At the end of an hour, Peebles's face was flushed with alcohol and excitement. Sure by now that his man was well-lubricated enough, Rory decided to change tactics. "I'm getting a little tired of cards," he said, dropping the deck onto the table top.

Peebles looked disappointed, then caught himself. "Well . . . it was time I got on home anyhow."

"Oh, the hell with home," Rory said carelessly. "I was thinking about something a little more . . . stimulating, like Madame Polly's."

Peebles's eyes showed renewed interest. Madam Polly's was the better of the two local whorehouses, a small establishment on the outskirts of town that boasted four rather nice-looking and fairly young women. Two different times since he'd arrived in town, Rory had noticed Peebles slipping into Polly's, rather furtively, as if afraid that his sainted mother would catch him at it. Rory recognized the innate caution in the other man's eyes, and thought for a moment that he might have lost him, might have pushed too fast.

But Rory had underestimated the progress he'd made. True, Peebles was the kind of man who preferred to sin secretly, but by now he'd conceived a high opinion of Rory Cavanaugh. Here was a man among men, one that other men instinctively respected, and he was asking him, John Peebles, to join him in an intimate act.

"Why sure . . . let's go," Peebles said, although his voice was a little breathless.

So they left the saloon together and walked down the street

toward Madame Polly's, Peebles more or less drunk by now,
Rory alertly sober, although he figured he was doing a pretty
good job of acting drunk. Peebles blathered on about his
miserable job while Rory chimed in from time to time,
choosing comments that would bolster the other man's self-
esteem.

Rory was well-known at Polly's; he'd already made several
very pleasant visits. The place was clean, as were the girls,
and he figured that they were high-priced enough to keep
away the town's potentially diseased riff-raff.

Polly herself greeted the two men as they walked into her
rather over-ornate living room. She smiled openly at Rory,
but frowned in surprise when she saw who was with him.
Although Peebles was an old customer, his usual style was
to come in when there was no one else in the living room,
ask for his regular girl, then disappear with her into a back
room.

But money is money, and Rory had shown himself to be a
big spender. "We'll have some drinks, Polly," he said jovial-
ly. "And two of your prettiest."

"Two apiece?" she asked coquettishly. Rory laughed up-
roariously, while Peebles looked stunned at the idea. "No
. . . we'll start with just one apiece," Rory replied, grinning.
"But later . . . who knows?" Along with the surprise, he
had seen fascination lurking behind Peebles's usually bland
expression.

Smiling professionally, Polly brought a bottle of what Rory
knew was fairly decent whiskey—reflected, unfortunately, by
the price. Polly was a rather round and rosy woman in her
late forties. Rory had been tempted by her, had even made
an offer, but Polly had turned him down. "Never for money,"
she'd said firmly. "Not any more. Now, it's only for love,
and I don't think that's what you have in mind, honey. I let
my girls bring in the cash."

However, she liked Rory, and wondered what he was doing
chumming it up with a rat like Peebles. The girl Peebles
always asked for had told her what a little shit he was in bed.

But he paid well, and that's what the girl was in it for, and unlike Polly she had no one else's body to sell but her own.

Out of habit, Polly called out Peebles's usual girl, a chubby, big-busted blonde in her early twenties named Sally. For Rory, she chose Kathy, a languid, dark-eyed brunette with a lithe, taut body. Polly was surprised when she caught a moment's regret in Peebles's eyes; in the past he had always rejected anyone but Sally. Obviously, Rory was wreaking all kinds of changes in Peebles's usually dull behavior.

Accepting Sally, Peebles was about to head off to a back room with her as usual, but Rory stopped him. "Let's have a few drinks out here together first, the four of us," he insisted. Peebles hesitated, then, as with so many other things today, he gave in to Rory's judgment.

Polly, anticipating other clients, insisted that they go into a small sitting room. There were two overstuffed couches in the room, facing each other only a few feet apart, with a low table between them. The bottles and glasses went onto the table. Then Rory and Kathy sat down across from Peebles and Sally.

Right from the first Rory was a laughing, rollicking ball of fun. While Peebles watched, Rory slid one hand up Kathy's slender thigh. The girl turned toward him, smiled into his face. Rory's hand went further up under her dress. Peebles noticed a quick grimace of shocked delight pass over Kathy's face as Rory did something pleasant to her.

A few minutes later Rory had the bodice of Kathy's dress down around her waist, and Peebles found himself looking at small, but perfectly-formed breasts. He had always chosen Sally because she had such big, white, soft breasts, but now he found himself admiring the other girl's lithe upper body, the dark nipples that tipped her naked breasts, the way her long dark hair slid back and forth over her bare shoulders.

Then Sally was pressing against him. "Do you want to play a little too, honey?" she asked huskily. She couldn't stand the little bastard, but when she made him feel good, he paid extra.

Peebles let Sally guide his hand down her cleavage, but he was only partially aware of the pillowy softness of her big breasts. He had never seen another man making love to a woman, and he wondered if he was going to now. This new friend of his, this Rory Cavanaugh, was doing one hell of a lot of things to his girl. Peebles had never had a friend like Rory before. Most of his relationships with other men involved only business. Like his relationship with Harlan Harrison. He knew that Harrison had no great love for him, or he for Harrison. They would tolerate one another only as long as the money continued to roll in.

But Rory, he was something else. Peebles had seen what he'd done to that man in the saloon, seen him play cards, watched him laugh at life. Obviously, Rory really knew how to live. And he'd invited him, John Peebles, to share some of that life with him.

Rory suddenly became aware of the lackluster way Peebles was fondling Sally, and of Peebles's fascination with his girl, Kathy. "Tell you what," he said. "What say we switch girls? You go ahead and take Kathy, and I'll swap for Sally."

He knew he'd struck pay dirt when he saw the mad gleam of excitement in Peebles's eyes. He'd hated to make the offer, he'd had more than one romp with Kathy and considered her a tiger in bed. And he wasn't in the mood for a fat blonde.

He was not alone in his regret. He saw from the look in Kathy's eyes that she was not eager to switch him for Peebles, which was flattering to Rory's ego, but Kathy was a whore and she would do it, and as for himself, he was not here for sex alone. He was here to get Peebles to trust him, to rely on him. He was here to use the intimacy of this situation to forge a manly bond between himself and Peebles, at least on Peebles's part, a bond that would place Peebles securely in his hands.

Then after that, God help the thieving, back-shooting little bastard.

CHAPTER SEVENTEEN

Rory had no guilt at all over his slow entrapment of John Peebles; he was doing what he loved, living on the edge. He had always lived on the edge. As a boy he had run with one of New York's toughest street gangs, not from necessity or poverty; his father made a good living, but from the sense of excitement engendered by constant street warfare. True, his father habitually ignored him, which Rory had resented, hell, he'd been hurt, although back then he'd never have admitted it to himself.

He could now. There were still memories of his mother and father lying dead on the prairie near their wrecked train. Nightmare images of the bloody red caps of their scalped heads, their staring, horrified eyes. He had pretended that that had not bothered him either. But it had.

By rights he should have hated Gabe; he'd been one of the men who'd attacked the train. But the expected hatred had never developed. From the very first he had felt an intense bond with Gabe, not just because he'd saved him from the Indians, hell, Gabe had looked like one of them, had *been* one of them, dressed in skins, daubed with war paint. There was no easy way to say just what it was that overcame the horror of it, but from that day on Gabe had been his lodestar, his guiding light.

He'd shown Rory a life of genuine adventure, infinitely more exciting than the youthful urban predations of his gang. Rory had become hooked, and knew that he'd die of boredom, probably actually die, if he were not able to do the fascinating things that he did with Gabe, such as trap this little rodent, Peebles. Rory, like Gabe, probably because of Gabe, despised men who used positions of power to cheat the weak. Peebles was part of a plot to steal food out of peoples' mouths, people who were starving to death. No, he felt no guilt at all over what he was doing to Peebles. Peebles was a shit.

In a way, at least in this caper, Rory fancied himself a detective, maybe even a great detective. One of his heroes had been that hoary old sleuth, Allen Pinkerton. Rory knew that he'd never work for the Pinkerton agency, he could not, even on a bad day, imagine himself actually working for anyone, letting others tell him what to do. Besides, the Pinkerton agency had begun to lean on people, little people, the poor. Rory did not appreciate that, not even a little bit.

Of course, he would not be able to keep up this masquerade for long, nor would he need to. Something had to break soon, and it did.

Rory was playing cards one day when Peebles came into the saloon. Rory immediately sensed that Peebles was even more nervous than usual. He nodded jerkily in Rory's direction, then went over to stand at the bar, where he immediately ordered a whiskey. He made no effort to join Rory, almost seemed embarrassed that Rory was there.

Peebles tossed off the first glass of whiskey and was working on his second when a man came into the saloon and walked up to Peebles. "Guess we should do a little talkin' 'fore you get too shit-faced," the man said, not exactly sneering, but giving that impression.

"Sure, Colonel," Peebles replied. "What about?"

"The next shipment."

Again Peebles swallowed nervously, his throat working. "I . . . dunno," he muttered.

The man looked at him fiercely. "You dunno what?" he snapped back.

"Well . . . it's getting risky."

The other man pinned Peebles with his eyes. "There's all kinds of ways it could get risky," he replied, his voice nasty.

"Okay . . . okay," Peebles said sulkily. "But you sure as hell ain't doin' too well yourself, about catching that Conrad son of a bitch." He tossed off the rest of his whiskey, and came close to glowering.

The other man looked a little surprised, as if he had prodded a puppy and it had snapped at him. "That bastard is long gone. Maybe even dead. There was blood all over the place where they last saw him. He probably crawled off into some hole to die. But what the hell are we doing talking about it in here? Let's go to your office."

Peebles had been in the middle of ordering another drink, but he cancelled the order and followed the other man out of the saloon. On the way to the door, one of the cowhands, there were always a few in the saloon, nodded to the newcomer. "Howdy, Colonel Harrison."

The man grunted some response that Rory could not quite make out and nodded back.

Rory whistled silently. So that was the great Colonel Harrison. Not much to look at. From first impressions he appeared to be a real four-flusher. He only looked good in comparison to Peebles, whom he obviously ran. But behind the surface impression of flakiness, Harrison gave off an unsettling aura of . . . well, why not say it? Of evil.

Rory would have loved to overhear what Peebles and Harrison were talking about in Peebles's office, but it was daylight, and he was not a fool, he'd be seen. But it would be night soon, and maybe he could stir things up a little. From his behavior in the saloon, Peebles was pretty badly strung out. Maybe it was time to give him a little push over the edge.

First he did a little scouting. In such a small town it was not difficult to discover that Harrison had taken a room in the local hotel, Rory's hotel. But he'd been dumb enough, at least in Rory's estimation, to take a room on the ground floor. The room had a window that faced out into the alley, just at the spot where the alley was darkest.

Peebles did not come to the saloon that night. Scouting again, Rory saw him sitting in the hotel dining room with Harrison, eating some of its awful swill. Rory had always figured that the greatest privation of the Wild West was not the Indians, nor the heat and cold, not even the fleas and lice. It was the awful food.

Peebles was slopping it up, all right. Rory had already discovered that the man would eat anything, apparently without tasting it, an advantage in this miserable burg. You could probably slip buffalo chips onto his plate and he wouldn't notice. Harrison seemed to be eating heartily enough, too. But then, he was a Texan, and Texans would eat anything. Rory loathed Texans.

Peebles had a small apartment behind his office. Knowing that Peebles and Harrison would probably remain in the hotel for some time, Rory figured it was the perfect time to provide a nice little surprise for Peebles. He slipped upstairs to get some things he'd already secreted in his room. Stuffing them into his pockets, he silently descended the back stairs.

There was no moon, and with the lack of municipal lighting, the night was blacker than a banker's heart. Slipping through alleyways, Rory approached the rear of Peebles's place. The primitive lock on the back door was no challenge at all for Rory's New York street skills. Within a minute, he was inside.

Wasting no time, he poured blood from a mason jar all over Peebles's pillow. He'd gotten the blood earlier in the day when some men had slaughtered a cow. Next, he took out a note he had written and laid it on the pillow, where it was least bloody. The note would soak up some of the blood, but not enough so that it could not be read.

The note was simple . . . and chilling. It read: "Peebles. The reservation is still hungry. I want the cattle. Now."

It was signed *Gabe Conrad*. Rory pinned the note to the pillow with a long thin butcher knife. Then he left the room, slipping back outside.

Rory had already scouted out a suitable place from which to watch. He did not wait long, Peebles came back about an hour later. Rory could see that he was a little unsteady on his feet. Drunk, as usual. Good. The booze would probably intensify his reaction.

Rory waited. A light came on inside the office; Peebles had gone in through the front door. Then the light moved toward the back of the building. Peebles was undoubtedly carrying a lamp back toward his sleeping quarters. Finally, the two small windows of the back room gave off a dim glow. Peebles was inside his bedroom.

It took longer than Rory had expected. Perhaps Peebles was digging a hidden bottle out of a drawer. Finally Rory heard it, a hoarse cry, a bellow of shock and fear.

A few seconds later Peebles came bursting out of the front door, moving fast. He did not even bother to shut the door. Rory was pretty sure that he could see a blur of white in Peebles's hand. The note.

Peebles headed straight for the hotel. Slipping along behind him, Rory ducked into the alley and positioned himself next to Harrison's window, pleased to see that the window was open a few inches. A faint glow shone through the curtains. Apparently Harrison was still up.

Rory heard a pounding on the room's door. "What the hell . . . ?" he heard Harrison say.

"Colonel . . . Colonel . . . it's me!" Peebles shouted from the hallway.

There was the sound of swift footsteps, then the opening of a door. "What the hell are you doing here at . . . ?" Harrison snarled.

"Look at this . . . look at this!" Peebles cut in. There was panic surging through his voice. A moment's silence followed; he must have handed the note to Harrison. Then Harrison's growl, "Son of a bitch!"

"He was right there! Right there in my room!" Peebles half-shouted. "If I'd been there, he could have killed me! Could have snuck up on me while I was asleep and cut my throat!"

"Shut up!" Harrison snarled. "You'll wake up the whole damned hotel. Here . . . have a drink."

The sound of glass clinking against glass. Then a moment later, Peebles's voice again, a little calmer now. "You said he was gone. Maybe dead. But he isn't, and he's after me. Me, not you."

Rory heard the sound of pacing, then Harrison's voice. "I'll start some patrols. If he comes near town again, we'll nail him for sure. I'll have Buck and Harry go around with you, guard your back."

When Peebles spoke again, he sounded almost resigned. "How long can they do that? How long before . . . ?"

"Long enough to get us through this next shipment!" Harrison replied sharply. "It's due in about three days, isn't it?"

"Yes . . . sure. But . . . ."

"No buts. When the cattle get here, drive them out toward the reservation, like you usually do. Use the same men, the ones I always provide you. The rendezvous point is going to be a little different this time. There's a small valley about ten miles out of town, where the stream branches right. You know the place, it's near that old Indian burial site."

"Yeah. I know the place. But, with Conrad running around loose, do you think it's safe . . . ?"

"I'll have my men scour the countryside first, all the way to the reservation. Once the cattle are out of your hands, you'll have nothing to worry about. My men'll meet you there in the valley. Split the herd up in the usual way, the usual divvy. The Indians can't count for shit. They won't know how many are missing, and even if they did, who the hell's going to listen to a bunch of dirty, lyin' savages?"

"Conrad did," Peebles said stubbornly. "I don't know how much longer we can do this. People are gonna . . . ."

When Harrison replied, his voice was ugly, full of menace. "You'll do it as long as I say you do it. You're in this deep, Peebles, and you like the money as much as I do. You'll get your usual cut, as soon as I move the cattle west into Montana and sell them to the mines. Those miners gotta eat, an' the mine owners pay top dollar. They don't waste time checkin' brands. Just move this load out, and maybe one more after that, then you can quit."

A bitter laugh from Peebles. "You've said that before. And then there's always one more. I don't understand you, Harrison. You're already a rich man. This is chicken feed . . . ."

"A man is never too rich, Peebles. Every little bit helps. Besides, it makes me happy to stick it to those redskins. Stop worrying about me. You just worry about your part. Get those cattle where I want them."

"All right, Harrison. If I live that long. What am I supposed to do? Go home and wait for that slippery son of a bitch to knife me in my sleep?"

Harrison chuckled. "What do you want *me* to do, Peebles? Have Buck tuck you in for the night?"

"That's not funny, Harrison." Rory detected the first signs of real resentment in Peebles's voice.

Harrison was aware of it, too, and he moved to soothe Peebles. "Nothing to worry about. I'll have some of the boys patrol the town, keep an eye on your place. Nobody's gonna knife you in your sleep."

There was a little more muttering from Peebles, but he seemed calmer now. Rory had to admit that Harrison was a smooth bastard. He listened for a little while more, as Harrison and Peebles talked over a few more details of the diversion of the annuity cattle that were supposed to go to the reservation. It sounded as if damned few of them would make it there. Rory was amazed by the sheer petty greed of it. And by Harrison's unconcern for the misery it would create.

Except that this time Harrison's plan wasn't going to work.

Not if Rory Cavanaugh and Gabe Conrad had anything to say about it.

Rory quietly slipped away from the window, moved down the alley, then quietly stole up the stairs to his room, where he spent ten minutes outfitting himself for the trail. He had some hard riding to do.

CHAPTER EIGHTEEN

"Do you really think you're well enough to ride?" Kate asked.

Gabe flexed his left shoulder, put weight on his right leg. "Well enough."

Seeing the concern on Kate's face, he smiled. "I'm used to getting shot. I heal a lot faster than I did the first time. You get tougher as you get older."

Rory had arrived at Kate's place a couple of hours before dawn, with news of the planned hijacking of annuity beef. "What do you figure?" Rory had asked after telling his tale.

"I'm going to stop them from stealing those cattle," Gabe replied. "Every head is going to end up on the reservation."

Rory's face lit up with excitement. "Great. When do we ride?"

Gabe shook his head. "Not you. Me. I think it's better that you stay in town, keep working on Peebles. We don't really have anything concrete on Harrison. If you're there, on the scene, maybe you can come up with some kind of proof."

Looking crestfallen, Rory had said stubbornly, "It's too big a job to do alone. You'll get yourself killed."

Gabe had smiled again. "I won't be alone."

After that, he said no more about it. He and Kate had seen Rory off after a hurried breakfast. Gabe was afraid that if Rory was away from town for too long, Peebles might get suspicious.

Now, with Rory gone, Gabe was preparing himself. Kate watched him clean and oil his guns. When he finally loaded them, she could not hide her concern any longer. "Don't go off like this. You'll get yourself killed."

When he looked up at her, there was something in his face that bothered her, an alienness. "Only the rocks live forever," he replied. His voice was flat, his face expressionless, and to her surprise she discovered that she was a little afraid of him. Maybe more than a little.

As he continued preparing himself, this sense of alienness deepened. She watched as he took a tied bundle of red horsehair from his saddlebag. He wove the horsehair into his long sandy hair. Then he drew from another saddlebag a buffalo hide coat. When he put it on she saw that it was very beautifully worked, soft and supple, glowing. There was a design high on the back, the stylized picture of a bird. "Oh, what a beautiful coat," she burst out. She pointed to the design on the back. "That's an Indian Thunderbird, isn't it?"

He nodded. He could sense the unasked questions inside her. But what could he say? How could he explain to this fine young woman these objects from another world? Nor did he want to. His mother had made the Thunderbird design after he had completed a vision quest. He had been Long Rider then. After four days of fasting and waiting on a hilltop, he had finally had a vision. A disturbing vision of personal loss, of separation from The People, of the very disappearance of The People themselves from the plains on which they lived.

At the end of that vision, the Thunderbird, the Winged God, *Wakinyan*, had appeared to him, had actually settled down across his back and shoulders, had guided him in further visions, and while *Wakinyan* had been with him, he had felt protected, invulnerable.

The Medicine Man, High Backbone, his mentor, had interpreted his dream, had foretold that he would one day walk among the whites. High Backbone had also told Long Rider that The Winged God would henceforth be his protector. Later, the old man had made the red horsehair broach for him, to be worn as a reminder of this protective power.

When Long Rider told his mother of his vision, she had been preparing and decorating a new buffalo hide tipi cover. Impressed by the vision, she had worked a yellow thunderbird into the tipi design. Quite an accomplishment for a former Boston Belle.

The new tipi cover had not lasted long. A few days later the soldiers had attacked the sleeping village. Both Long Rider's mother, and his new wife, Yellow Buckskin Girl, had been killed. After the fight, the soldiers had burned the tipis and the food supply, so that The People would die of hunger and cold during the coming winter. Returning to the village after the soldiers left, Long Rider had discovered that the only part of the new tipi cover that had not been burnt was a large section that contained the Thunderbird painting.

After he had buried his mother and wife and stepfather, Long Rider had taken the unburnt section away, and later fashioned it into the coat he was now wearing. He usually wore the coat when danger was imminent. The design on the coat, the long wings of *Wakinyan*, covering his shoulders and back, gave him the same sense of power and protection as when the Winged One had been riding his shoulders during the original vision. It was a coat made for war.

No, it would be foolish to try and tell all this to Kate, nor to any other white person. Rory knew some of it, but only some.

Finally ready, Gabe picked up his gear and weapons and went outside. Juan had already saddled his horse. Putting the saddlebags in place, and ramming his rifles into their saddle scabbards, Gabe mounted. Kate stood below him, totally aware of how impressive he looked mounted on his horse, the Thunderbird coat on his back, his hair cascading over his shoulders. With that cold fire shining from those pale gray eyes, and the hawklike face, he was the total man of war.

He nodded to her. How remote he seemed. "Thank you," he said. "You saved my life."

She tried some humor. "And you saved me from a fate worse than death."

He did not seem to understand. He only nodded again, then turned his mount and rode out of the yard. Kate remained in place, looking after him until he'd disappeared into a patch of trees. "Goddamn you," she murmured to herself. "You come back to me, Gabe Conrad."

But the man who rode away was no longer Gabe Conrad. With the Thunderbird coat on his back, and the red horsehair in his hair, he was once again Long Rider, the Oglala warrior. And he was on the warpath. This was no time to think of women, or to think of the past. He was going into battle.

But there were things to be done before he was ready to face battle. He'd been among the white men too long, his *ni*, his spirit had been soiled, weakened. It must be renewed if he were to find the strength to survive. And he must do this in the Lakota way. He must purify himself with *inipi*.

He rode up into some hills, looking for the right kind of place. He finally found it near a small stream. Dismounting, he tied his horse with a long leadrope in a place where it would be able to find grass. Then he spent an hour hunting up a dozen small stones four or five inches thick. He was painstaking in his selection, careful to avoid stones that might either crumble or explode in the heat.

Then he began to gather wood, dry wood that would not smoke when burned, and thus give away his location. In the spot he had selected, he laid four good-sized pieces of wood pointing east-west, then four more on top pointing north-south. He then piled the stones on top of the wood and set the wood on fire.

While the stones heated, Long Rider went down close to the stream and cut himself seven lengths of willow saplings. He brought the saplings back near where the fire was burning and, using his bowie, dug out seven small holes in a circle a little wider across than a man is tall.

While the stones heated, Long Rider patiently peeled the bark from the saplings. When they had been peeled white and clean, Long Rider stuck the butt ends of the saplings into the holes and tamped dirt around them. Then he scooped out a shallow hole in the center of the circle. This was where he would place the rocks when they had heated sufficiently.

Using the strips of bark, he began tying the upper ends of the saplings together, until he had formed the skeleton of a sweat lodge, a dome about four feet high. He then roamed about the area, pulling up several clumps of sage, which he spread across the north side of the interior of the sweat lodge.

He did not have enough animal skins to cover the sweat lodge, so he used what he had; his blankets, some of his extra clothing, and even his Thunderbird coat. When he had made the sweat lodge as airtight as he could, he went over to the fire and checked the stones. They were glowing with an almost white heat. Cutting a pair of forked sticks, he carried the stones one by one into the sweat lodge, depositing them into their central pit. He also carried a few coals inside and put them on top of the rocks, then stacked some of the sage close to the pit, so that he could burn it for its sweet smoke.

He then took off all his clothing, and, taking his pipe and his water bag, crawled naked into the sweat lodge. Pulling a portion of blanket across the opening, he settled himself on some of the sage he had laid down, and waited as his eyes slowly adjusted to the darkness. There was a little light coming from the coals, and a little more from poorly-sealed joints in the sweat lodge covering.

While he waited for his eyes to adjust, he filled and lit the pipe, performing the usual ritual. The smoke felt good going into him. After he had smoked, he threw some of the sage onto the fire. It began to burn, and he inhaled its smoke too.

A few minutes later the coals winked out, leaving only the dark red glow of the hot stones. He poured some of his water over his head and face, then, using a crude dipper he had made out of twigs, he sprinkled water over the stones. The water hissed and spat, and steam immediately began to fill the sweat lodge.

He sprinkled water on the stones four times in all. The second time there was a sharp report, like a rifle shot. One of the stones must have split. The steam became thicker, hot, alive, pressing in on him. Breathing was difficult, the steam seared his throat.

Sweat poured from his face and body. His eyes stung, he was blinded. The smell of burning sage coated his tongue. The urge to escape, to go outside into the clean cool air, was very powerful.

But Long Rider remained seated, chanting sacred songs, asking The Great Spirit and The Winged One to hear him, to grant him purity and strength.

As the steam diminished again, he sprinkled water on the stones for the third time. There was less of an effect; the stones were cooling, but they still produced steam, clouds of searing, purifying steam.

When he finally sprinkled water on the stones the fourth and last time, he felt a sense of peace, of well-being, begin to suffuse his person. He prayed once more for the wisdom and power to accomplish this thing he was about to do.

He knew when it was time, when it was enough. He gathered up his water bag and pipe and crawled from the lodge out into the open. Running to the stream, he plunged into its coolness. He lay quietly in the water, letting it flow over him, feeling free, floating, strong.

He got up from the stream, and dried and dressed himself. Then he pulled down the sweat lodge and scattered its components. Finally satisfied, he retrieved his horse—which did not want to be taken away from all that rich grass—and rode off, and as he rode, he knew that he was complete again, that his *ni*, the energy that he took inside himself the way a man breathed air, was strong and pure again, and that all was right with the world.

He had lived many years among the white men, he'd been

taught their ways by both Rory Cavanaugh and by his Boston grandfather. He'd been reading his mother's Bible since boyhood. He knew what the white man's world had to offer, but in all his years he'd never yet found among their ways anything that had more to offer than what he'd grown up with, the Lakota way, the way of oneness with the earth and sky and wind and water. The way of completeness.

And, once again complete, once again Long Rider, with Gabe Conrad buried somewhere in the background, he headed toward the last village of his People, the Oglala Lakota, to fight for them as he had fought for them in the old days, when the buffalo covered the earth from horizon to horizon, when the earth had still been free of the white man's mechanical chains.

CHAPTER NINETEEN

Long Rider was able to get far too close to the village without being noticed. That disturbed him; there were no scouts, no warning system. It was the same situation that had cost him his mother and his wife that terrible morning, years ago, when the soldiers had been able to ride right up to the Arapahoe camp where they were temporarily staying, even after the camp had been warned by a warrior and his wife, who were passing through, that they had seen soldiers not far away. No wonder the whites had so consistently triumphed.

However, the reception he received when he rode into the village warmed his heart. Children jumped up and down, women trilled a welcome, and the men came out of their lodges, dignified but smiling, with Tall Bear in the lead. "Welcome, Long Rider," Tall Bear said. "Come into my lodge. The women will care for your horse."

Once in the lodge, with the principal men grouped around the fire, and with Long Rider seated in the place of honor, facing the doorway, the pipe was passed. As custom demanded not much was said at first, it was, after all, a solemn occasion, this passing of the pipe. But after a few minutes had gone by, Long Rider realized that the quality of the si-

lence was subtly different than it had been during his last
visit. The men were looking at him strangely. "What is it,
my friends?" he asked. "I can tell that something is bothering you."

The men looked around at one another, then arrived at an
unspoken consensus. It was Tall Bear who finally spoke. "It
is not as if there is something wrong," he said with a sigh.
"Perhaps it is simply that something is right. We see a change
in you, something that was not there before. We see, my
friend, something from the old days. We see a warrior."

Long Rider nodded. "It is true. For at least a little while
I have washed away, with *inipi*, some of the white ways that
have slowly been invading my spirit. I have done this because
there is a path to ride. The path of war."

He told them, then, about Peebles and Harrison and the
annuity beef that would soon be on its way. There were smiles
at the thought of meat, then frowns when he told them that
Peebles and Harrison planned to steal most of the meat.

"But you have not come here to tell us of disaster," Tall
Bear said. "You have a plan."

"Yes. The cattle will not be stolen. But to accomplish this
I will need four men from the village to ride with me. Do
you have horses for four men?"

Tall Bear looked worried. "We do. But are you saying that
we must go to war with the whites again? Are we to chance
being completely destroyed?"

"No," Long Rider replied. "I am the only one who will
war against the whites, and since I am, at least in their
eyes, a white man too, they will have no reason to attack
The People."

He described his plan. The men were pleased by its clev-
erness, and by its traditional nature, which involved the stealing away of another's animals, a symbolic counting of coup,
a game from the old days, played out again. But they were
also embarrassed, ashamed that none of them but Long Rider
would be able to fight openly against the men who were rob-
bing them.

Nevertheless, they accepted Long Rider's plan. A few minutes later they all went outside, where Tall Bear called together four young men. They were thin from hunger, and apathetic from being penned up and useless on the reservation. But they came alive when Tall Bear told them of the plan. They broke out in loud yips of excitement, and began dancing the war dance.

"Silence!" Long Rider shouted. The men were so surprised by his lack of politeness that they did indeed fall silent.

"You must listen, and listen well. Then after you have heard what I have to say, you must decide again whether you want to ride with me."

To build up a sense of drama, Long Rider let several seconds pass before he continued. "You will not fight. You will not even take weapons. You will not wear war paint, you will not make the slightest sound, any sound that would tell the white men that you are there. They will see only me. Do you understand?"

There were shocked looks from two of the young men, sullen growls from the other two. This was intolerable. Oglala warriors went to war as independents. War chiefs led only by example, they had no binding power, they could not give direct orders. If an individual warrior grew tired of fighting, he simply left the battlefield. If he decided to fight using a different strategy, he simply did so. Long Rider fully realized that this was one of the many reasons why the whites, with their greater discipline, had won so consistently.

"If you do not do as I say," he continued, "it is The People who will suffer. The soldiers will come and kill them all, men, women, and children. You have seen this happen many times in the past, but it will not happen this time, because I will take no one with me who will not promise to do as I have spoken."

He looked from man to man, all four in turn, staring directly into their eyes, a sign of challenge among the Oglala. "Do you agree?" he demanded.

The men muttered among themselves, and one refused to

ride with Long Rider, considering the conditions too onerous. Another young man was found to take his place, the boy who had been with the old man and the women when Long Rider had surprised and killed the white men who had attacked them.

"Good," Long Rider said to his four volunteers. "But once again I must warn you. If any among you does not do exactly as I say, I will kill that man on the spot. I will kill him to ensure the safety of the village."

He was relieved to see all four men nod solemnly. They knew he meant it. They would do as he said.

They rode out early the next morning. Long Rider set a slow pace. The horses, with the exception of his own, were sorry nags; he wanted to save their strength for the big effort that would come later in the day.

As they rode along, watching the skyline, taking advantage of every bit of cover, Long Rider felt the years slip away. How good it was to be riding once again with Oglala warriors, even with these four untried young men. If he forgot the intervening years, he might imagine that they were on their way to raid their old enemies, the Crow, to steal horses or women or both. Today might be a day to count coup, to do the things that made a man a man, things that quickened the blood, things that made of life a never-ending adventure. Ah, but never again. Not truly in the old way.

About ten o'clock they saw a distant cloud of dust. "The herd," Long Rider said.

They rode even more carefully now. Half an hour later they caught sight of Peebles and the cattle. Taking cover behind a screen of thick brush at the top of a rise, with one man holding all five horses a hundred yards back, they carefully studied the scene below. Long Rider was quite surprised; he had not expected so many cattle. There must be two hundred head. Then it occured to him that it was not only the reservation that Peebles and Harrison were cheating, it was the government, too. Peebles was probably reporting many more Indians on the reservation than there actually were, and thus

drawing a much larger annuity payment. Long Rider began
to wonder how many other things Peebles was stealing . . .
flour, supplies, blankets, money itself.

One of the Oglala touched his arm. "More white men are
coming from the other direction," he whispered.

From their hilltop they watched four men ride toward Peebles and the herd. Using his night glasses, Long Rider studied
the four men. Two appeared to be ordinary cowhands, lightly
armed, happy-go-lucky. The other two looked more like gunmen; they were heavily armed and rode warily. They would
be real danger.

He watched while Peebles and the four men conferred.
Then the herd was divided. It was quite a breathtaking divi-
sion; the four newcomers cut out the bulk of the herd, about
a hundred and fifty animals, and begin driving them away to
the northwest, the general direction of Harrison's ranch. The
size of the theft angered Long Rider. He tried to study Peebles's face through the glasses, but the distance was too great
to make out facial expressions. He sensed, however, from the
stiff way Peebles sat his saddle, that he was under considerable tension. Rory had told Long Rider what he'd done to
Peebles. Good. A frightened man is a man liable to make
mistakes.

Long Rider moved his four men down off the hill. All five
of them remounted and began to shadow the four hands with
the hundred and fifty stolen head. "We must let them get far
from the others, so that they cannot call for help," Long
Rider said.

Now the horses would have to be pushed harder, it was
imperative that they get well ahead of the herd, so that an
ambush could be set up, a one-man ambush.

About two in the afternoon Long Rider found the kind of
terrain he was looking for, a valley that narrowed suitably,
then opened out again in such a way that it was impossible
to see beyond the narrow choke point. His four men were to
be placed just the other side of the choke point. "Remember," he warned them. "You must not be seen. If there is

killing here, and I think that there will be killing, then it is important that the only one to blame for that killing is the white man, Gabe Conrad, not Oglala warriors.''

The young men reluctantly agreed. ''If I am not successful,'' Long Rider added, ''if I am killed, then ride quickly for home. Do not attempt to help me.''

More glum nods, but Long Rider was almost certain that they would obey. He solemnly touched the shoulder of each man. Then it was time to separate. The men rode away through the gap, and took up positions in the brush where the valley widened out again. After checking to made certain that they were not visible, Long Rider turned and rode back toward the white men and the approaching herd.

He rode around them in a half-circle, so that he could approach them from one side. He was only fifty yards away when they finally saw him, sitting his horse quietly, both hands on his saddle horn. ''Jesus!'' one of the cowhands burst out. ''Who the hell are you?''

Long Rider let a few seconds pass in silence. Tension built. The four riders had bunched up, and the herd was stringing out a little. ''The name's Conrad,'' he finally said, his voice quiet, but carrying clearly. ''Gabe Conrad. You may have heard of me.''

Unimpressed, one of the gunhand-types smiled and scratched his head. ''Well I'll be damned. I thought we'd fixed your wagon for good.''

''Obviously not,'' Gabe replied. ''Now . . . you have something I want.''

''No, I don't think so,'' the same man replied. He was sitting his horse easily, apparently relaxed, but there was little doubt in Long Rider's mind that the man would fight. And that he would be a dangerous opponent.

Long Rider pointed to the cattle. ''Those are stolen animals. They belong on the reservation, all of them. I'm going to take them there. If you resist, I'll have to kill you.''

The gunhand shifted his weight slightly in the saddle. ''Well, well, well,'' he said, grinning. ''You and who else?''

The other gunhand had ridden up alongside him. He was less relaxed; his right hand was lying lightly on the butt of his Winchester. The other two men, the cowhands, were beginning to worry about the herd, which was milling about aimlessly. "Hey," one of them sang out. "We oughta be gettin' back to work."

"Shut up, Curly," the first gunhand snapped. "We got some other work to do first."

"Wait a minute," the second cowhand cut in. "Are these cattle really stolen?"

"Yeah," the other cowhand said. "I was wonderin' about that, too. Kinda strange, the way we cut 'em out from the other herd. I don't' want no part o' rustlin'. A man could get his neck stretched, rustlin'."

"Then ride back to your ranch," Long Rider warned the man. "This is not your fight. And when you get to the ranch, tell Harrison that he will not steal any more reservation beef. Ride now, while you still have the chance."

"Fuck you, Injun-lover!" one of the gunmen shouted. He was reaching for his rifle even as he spoke, but Long Rider was faster. His Winchester, while still in its saddle scabbard, was already cocked, and he had placed himself in the best possible position for drawing it quickly. He had the rifle out of its scabbard and firing before the other man could bring his own rifle into position. Long Rider blasted the other man out of the saddle with two quick shots.

The second gunman had gone for his rifle too, but as the man Long Rider had already shot fell from his saddle, his rifle discharged into the ground, scattering gravel against the belly of the second man's horse. The horse shied violently, throwing off the man's aim, and while he was able to get off a shot, his bullet missed Long Rider by more than a yard.

Long Rider slammed his heels against his horse's ribs, and rode in hard, firing quickly, zigzagging his mount back and forth. His next shot missed, but his third hit the second gunman in the throat. As the man began to fall, gagging on his own blood, Long Rider shot him through the chest.

The two cowhands had reacted much more slowly. One of them had his rifle half out of its saddle scabbard, and the other was thinking about it, but by then Long Rider was right in amongst them. They found themselves staring down the barrel of his smoking rifle. "If you fight, you'll die," he warned them, his voice whip-crack hard.

"Jesus," one of the cowhands murmured. He stared down at the two fallen gunhands, saw their blood soaking into the ground. They looked very dead.

Then he looked up again at Long Rider, mesmerized by the cold killing light deep inside those icy gray eyes.

"Or you can choose to ride away in peace," Long Rider continued. "Do as I have suggested. Go back to the ranch and tell Harrison what I told you to tell him . . . that I have taken the cattle to where they belong, and that there will be no more thefts."

The cowboy let his Winchester slip back into its scabbard. "Hell, you got us cold, mister. And like you said, it ain't our fight."

He looked over at his companion. "How 'bout you, Bill?"

Bill nodded. "Like you said. It ain't our fight. We ride."

Curly, the other man, looked down at the two dead gunhands. "Let the bastards lie there," he muttered. "Never could stand either one o' those two yahoos."

They turned their horses and rode away. Long Rider watched them go. When he was certain that they would not turn back, perhaps try to bushwack him, he spurred his horse toward the herd, firing into the air and shouting. The cattle, already spooked by the earlier shooting and the smell of blood, now panicked completely, stampeding down the valley, running full-tilt toward the point where it narrowed.

Now it was time for the four young Oglala to do their part; Long Rider would never have been able to get the cattle under control by himself; they would have scattered away over the countryside. But there were four superb riders posted on the far side of the choke point, and as the cattle came pouring through, the four young men closed in from the sides, forcing them to come together once again as a herd.

For a while it was pure madness. Long Rider was aware of the look of exultation on the faces of the men as they rode alongside the cattle. It was the same exultation he'd seen years before, when the Lakota had hunted the buffalo, when they had delighted in racing alongside for the kill, the old days when the killing madness swept over every man, and the hunters fired again and again into running, panicked animals.

Perhaps if he'd let these wild young men come armed they would have lost their heads, the old killing madness would have swept away their reason, and they would have shot down many of the cattle, out here, far from the reservation that now imprisoned not only their bodies, but their spirits as well.

The cattle ran hard, but within a few miles the four young men, with Long Rider bringing up the rear, had them under control. The tired animals slowed to a shambling walk. Long Rider knew that they needed rest, but he insisted that they be kept moving. It was important that they reach the village by nightfall.

Peebles did not push his own much smaller herd nearly as hard. He camped for the night about two hours' ride from the village. For Peebles, it was not a pleasant night. Still nervous, still remembering the hideous sight of his blood-soaked pillow with that knife sticking out of it, he slept poorly. Although he had five men with him, he kept expecting that crazy man, Conrad, to come crawling up on his bedroll like an Indian. And then he would feel the icy steel against his throat, feel his own blood pouring out onto the ground.

They pushed on early, and Peebles felt greatly relieved when they finally came in sight of the village. Then his relief changed to confusion. He had expected the usual sullen encampment, had expected a beaten people, had expected to see the hungry, desperate looks on their faces when they saw that he was bringing them cattle, meat. He had counted on that hunger, hoping that their relief when they saw food on the way would blunt their critical facilities, would keep them from wondering why there were so few cattle.

But this was not the camp of a starving people. To his amazement he saw huge hunks of meat sizzling over open fires, saw stew pots bubbling, saw happy children with bulging bellies and grease-smeared faces. Half a dozen beef hides were staked out on the ground, where the women were busy scraping the fat from the soft inner surface.

He saw, then, a herd milling about in a rope pen two hundred yards away. A feeling of premonition swept over him, and spurring his horse, he rode over toward the penned cattle. A quick check of the brands confirmed the worst. These were the same cattle he'd sent away with Harrison's four riders.

White with rage, Peebles galloped his horse back into the village. "Tall Bear!" he shouted. "Where the hell are you, you thieving redskin?"

Tall Bear came out of his tipi, calm, relaxed, erect, a blanket wrapped around his upper body. "Agent Peebles," he said calmly. "I am surprised. You have brought us even more beef."

Peebles was almost inchoherent. "What is this?" he screamed. "What is the meaning of this? What are those cattle doing over there?"

He was pointing with a trembling hand toward the penned cattle. "Why . . . they were brought in last night," Tall Bear replied. Then he pointed toward Peebles's smaller herd. "I am very much surprised to see you here this morning . . . bringing all these extra cattle. You are very generous."

The chief's very coolness and apparent surprise confused Peebles even more. "But who brought them?" he burst out. "Who the hell brought you all those other animals?"

"Why . . . a white man," Tall Bear replied, as if it were a foolish question, as if to say, who else but the whites could provide for his people?

My God, Peebles thought. Had Harrison double-crossed

him? "But who?" Peebles bleated. "For God's sake, what was his name?"

And then it came, the name he had been half-expecting, but nevertheless dreaded to hear. "He said his name was Conrad," Tall Bear replied, his voice calm, friendly. "Gabe Conrad. He must be a very good friend of yours, Mr. Peebles, because he insisted that we remember his name, that we tell it to you. And that we give you his message."

"Message?" Peebles asked weakly.

Tall Bear felt exultation sweep through him, but he hid it beneath his usual steady composure. "Yes," Tall Bear replied. "He said to tell you that he will be coming to see you."

And seeing the stricken look on Peebles terrified face, he could not help adding, "He said that it will be soon. Very soon."

CHAPTER TWENTY

For the first time since he'd come to town, Rory found himself fidgeting over his cards. He played cards for money, not for the love of it, which was, perhaps, one of the reasons he won consistently; he was not a gambler.

Besides, he had plenty of money now. Perhaps it was a half-realized desire to get this particular game over with that prompted him to forget his usual strategy of not winning big during any one game. Perhaps it was the character of the man he was playing against, a loud-mouthed cattle dealer from Fort Worth, who thought that he knew everything about cards worth knowing, and who wanted everyone else to hear about it.

Rory took pleasure in whittling the cattle dealer down to size. The more Rory won, the more the man fumed and swore, and the darker his face grew. Eventually there was over five hundred dollars on the table, with only Rory and the cattleman still in the game. Rory had artfully strung out the betting, seeming timid at times, impulsive at others.

Finally, after the freely sweating cattleman had made his last fifty dollar bet, Rory said the critical words, ''I call. Let's see those magic cards you're holding.'

Clay Dawson

Which was when Rory discovered that the man had been sweating because he was afraid Rory would not let the pot get high enough. The cattle buyer's face now shone red with triumph as he spread out his hand. It was a good hand: four sevens.

For several long seconds Rory made no move. His face even redder, the cattleman reached out for the pot. "Don't you want to see my hand first?" Rory asked sweetly.

The cattleman hesitated. Then an awful possibility began to occur to him. That possibility was realized when Rory laid out his cards, slowly, one by one, in ascending order. A ten-high straight flush. "Just push the money a little closer this way," Rory said casually.

The cattleman's face turned white. Then red again. "Why . . . you four-flushin' tinhorn gambler," he snarled. "You been pickin' away at me all afternoon, and at every other man who's had the misfortune to be sittin' across this table from you. Down where I come from, we . . . ."

"But we aren't down where you come from," Rory cut in lazily. How he detested men with big mouths. "Up here, most of the people can read and write. And they take baths more than once a month."

The man's face turned white again, then went through its usual change to red. He abruptly stood up, so quickly that his chair crashed over backwards. "You shit-eatin' prick," he snarled. "It's time somebody let a little air into your rotten carcass."

He was wearing a big Colt revolver strapped to his right hip. He was already making a motion toward the pistol's butt when Rory stood up too. But when Rory stood up, it was not so much an abrupt motion as a smooth and flowing one.

And as he stood, his right hand dipped beneath the left lapel of his coat, and came out holding his little .32 Smith and Wesson. While nothing was rushed, the entire series of movements took up very little time, and just as the cattleman's hand was settling around the butt of his .45, he found himself staring down his nose into the muzzle of a pistol.

He hesitated. The hole in the end of that barrel wasn't very big, but it was awfully close. He could imagine that little hunk of lead tearing up through his sinuses and scrambling his brains. So he froze.

"I do hate a bad loser," Rory said. Beneath its surface calmness, his voice was no longer pleasant.

By now all the fire had gone out of the cattleman. "No offense," he muttered, letting his hand slide away from his pistol butt. He nodded jerkily, then walked quickly from the saloon, never looking back.

Rory sat down again, and began raking in that big pot. It weighed his pockets down. He hated the feel of it. Hated the feel of this whole Goddamned town. A premonition swept over him, a feeling that the entire thing was starting to go bad. Why didn't he and Gabe just shoot a few holes in those two assholes, Peebles and Harrison, and ride on out?

Of course, he knew the answer to that; both Peebles and Harrison were men of consequence. Gun them down, and he and Gabe would be wanted murderers. Somehow, he'd have to get the goods on those thieving bastards.

Speak of the devil. Peebles chose that moment to walk into the saloon. Usually, he came right over to Rory, but this time he didn't even seem to notice that Rory was there, didn't notice that anyone was there, just walked over to the bar, ordered a big glass of whiskey, belted it down, and ordered another. And as he drank, his hands were shaking. John Peebles had had a very bad day.

A bad couple of days. First there'd been the shock of finding those cattle on the reservation, cattle meant for himself and Harrison. He'd had to watch them being eaten by those savages. And then that terrifying message from Conrad. Coming to get him. Coming soon.

Harrison's reaction to the loss of the cattle had not helped Peebles's state of mind at all. It had been out of all proportion to the dollar loss, an uncontrolled outburst of rage and hatred, a screaming monologue that had frightened Peebles. "I'll kill him!" Harrison had screamed. "I'll kill 'em all! Those fuck-

ing redskins, too! I know right down to my bones that they
were in this with Conrad, thicker'n thieves!''

The two cowhands who had brought back the story of the
theft of the cattle, or perhaps it might be fairer to say, their
rescue, had prudently left the area before their employer's
wrath could focus on them. So Peebles had had to bear the
brunt of that awesome outburst all by himself. As he downed
his second drink, he was still shaking from Harrison's tongue-
lashing.

Someone was standing next to him. He could sense a physical presence close to his elbow. An irrational fear that it
might be Gabe Conrad flashed through Peebles's mind, and
he spun in that direction.

Only to see his friend Rory Cavanaugh leaning against the
bar a couple of feet away, looking at him with what seemed
genuine concern. ''You look kind of peaked, John,'' Rory
said. ''Something bothering you?''

Thank God. Here was a friend. How Peebles needed a
friend.

They drank. And drank. Rory tried to moderate his own
drinking, while encouraging Peebles to put down more and
more of the hard stuff. But he had to drink hard, too, just to
keep up the mood, a mood of release, of shared confidences.
The moment he had seen the state Peebles was in, he'd sensed
that this was the time to make the big move. The moment to
nail the lid shut on Peebles and his boss.

After they'd spent a couple of hours in the bar, Rory helped
Peebles over to his place. They drank in the front office,
behind a locked door; Peebles seemed to have an aversion to
going into his bedroom. Eventually, with no one but Rory
present, Peebles began to open up more and more, to talk
about things he shouldn't have talked about. But why not? He
was with his friend, and he needed to talk.

He brought out the story of the cattle thefts bit by bit.
When he saw that each successive revelation seemed to faze
Rory not at all, he'd go on to the next, until he'd told the
whole thing. But always with Harrison the villain, of course,

the instigator, as if he'd roped Peebles into it, kicking and screaming, as if Peebles's own greed had not been enough to motivate him to betray his oath of office, to steal food from the mouths of people who needed it desperately.

Rory began to hate what he was doing, he felt as if he were wading knee-deep through shit. But he persevered, and eventually he was glad he did. Sobering up a little, Peebles gave him news that made the whole thing worth while. "More trouble coming," Peebles muttered. "Harrison's gonna get us both hung. Killing. Going to be a lot of killing." Then he laughed. "No, it ain't true. We ain't gonna hang. Nobody ever got hung for killing Indians."

He told Rory how Harrison, enraged over the loss of the beef, but even more over his loss of face, had decided that if he couldn't quite manage to settle the score with Gabe Conrad, he'd settle for taking it out on the tribe. Tomorrow, or the day after, he intended sending some men out onto the reservation, with orders to kill any Indians they came across, men, women or children.

"It could still bounce back on you," Rory said, his expression worried. "You're the Indian agent, you're the one responsible. If the truth ever came out it'd be easy for Harrison to lay the whole thing in your lap, then walk away scot-free."

"You really think so?" Peebles asked, immediately worried again.

"Yeah. He'd use you."

Peebles gnawed his lip. "Well . . . what the hell can I do?"

Rory appeared to mull it over for a while. Then his face lit up, as if with great inspiration. "I know! I have a friend back East, a big Boston lawyer. You could use him to cover yourself."

"How?" Peebles asked breathlessly.

"You'll write a letter, a legal document. You can write down all you've told me, the whole story, including dates, amounts, a very careful description of all that Harrison has done. We'll send it to this lawyer in a sealed envelope."

Peebles face went white. "Oh, God. Harrison would kill me if he ever found out."

"Uh-uh. We give the lawyer orders to open the letter only if anything happens to you. Any . . . accidents. That way, if you start suspecting Harrison of moving in on you, all you have to do is tell him about the letter, that any harm to you is going to cause one hell of a lot of harm to him, too. Then he won't dare make a move. You'll have the upper hand."

Maybe that was finally what did it . . . the idea of finally having the upper hand over Colonel Harlan Harrison. Or maybe it was simply the whiskey, but Peebles immediately sat down and wrote out a four page letter, detailing his illegal dealings with Harrison. He was still cagey enough to sit by himself behind his desk, guarding the actual words from Rory's view as he wrote, then stupid enough to hand the letter to Rory after sealing it inside an envelope. "You make sure your lawyer friend gets it," he said drunkenly. "Then I'll have me a real ace in the hole if that bastard Harrison tries to lean on me again."

He passed out half an hour later, after muttering more maledictions against Harrison. Rory dragged him into the bedroom, and lay him down on the bed, still fully clothed. He felt something akin to pity as he looked down at this weak, greedy little man.

Uh-Uh. Add the word vicious. When he'd recounted Harrison's plan to butcher him some Indians, Peebles had had no regret at all that innocent people were going to die. He'd only been concerned for his own skin. Let him rot in hell, Rory decided.

But right now, if innocent blood were not to flow, he had miles to cover.

CHAPTER TWENTY-ONE

The six men made camp just short of the reservation boundary. All were heavily armed, and all in a jovial mood, the joviality of men out on a hunting vacation. And as men will do on a hunting vacation, they were seated around their campfire, drinking heavily. Perhaps they were drinking so heavily because of the nature of the game they were after. Perhaps only because they liked drinking.

"I wanna get me a crack at one of them young squaws 'fore I draw blood," one man said. His name was Pete.

"Yeah. Get a crack at her 'fore you draw *her* blood," another replied, staring moodily at the bottle he had been drinking from. He was not completely comfortable with this assignment—killing Indians because they'd gotten under his boss's skin. But Colonel Harrison paid well, so if he said to go out and shoot up a few Indians, then by damn, he'd shoot up a few Indians. It wasn't like they were going to be shooting up any white people. But he figured he'd maybe do that, too, if Harrison paid him enough.

He didn't like the idea of killing any kids, though, Indian or not. He'd let his companions take care of that. He knew that Jack would be happy enough to take up any slack in that direction. He looked across at Jack. The firelight was casting moving shadows over his face. It was one hell of a hard face. Jack loved killing. He'd kill anything.

Jack was talking. "So," he said a trifle thickly—he'd been hitting the bottle pretty hard; maybe he was a little nervous about this thing, too. "We just ride out onto the reservation bold as brass. They ain't got many guns out there. We pick off any we see along the way, then when we get to the village, we lay off a few hundred yards and weed 'em out with our buffalo guns. If they come after us, we just ride away. I hear that their horses are in even worse shape than their guns."

"I still want me a crack at one of them young squaws," Pete said again. "A real young one. One that hasn't had any kids yet."

Jack guffawed. "That'll make her about twelve years old."

"That's okay by me."

Pete suddenly stiffened. "Hey! Who in the hell is that?"

The men all sprang to their feet. They had built a bright fire, which, although there was a moon, made the surrounding night seem all that much darker. But out at the limits of the firelight every one of them could see the dim figure of a man, standing close to the edge of the trees and brush that grew up on one side of the camp.

"Jesus," Pete muttered. "I wonder if them damn Injuns got wind of this thing. Maybe they're all around us."

It was this possibility, the suspicion that they might be surrounded, that kept the men from immediately snatching up their weapons and opening fire on the shadowy figure.

Then the man called out, "I saw your fire."

Pete sighed in relief. "It's a white man. Nothin' to work up a sweat over."

The stranger walked slowly toward the fire. The waiting men noticed that he wore a coat made of some kind of leather. And that he had long, sandy-colored hair. And that the firelight reflected from his eyes in a peculiar way.

However, he was not carrying a rifle, he seemed only to have a single pistol riding butt-forward on his right hip, so

they relaxed. "Come on over and share our fire, mister,"
Pete sang out, made mellow by the whiskey he'd drunk.

The man came closer, until he was only a couple of feet
away from Pete. Now Pete could see why the firelight had
looked strange reflecting from his eyes. They were very pale
eyes. Scary eyes. Pete instinctively took a step backwards.

"I'm afraid that I won't be able to share the fire with you,"
the stranger replied. "You see . . . I know why you're here."

Jack stepped forward aggressively. "Yeah? And who the
hell told you?"

"The wind," the man answered. "And I cannot share your
fire because I don't share fires with murderers of women and
children. I don't share fires with men I'm about to kill. I'm
here to stop you."

The man had spoken in a quiet and reasonable voice, and
since the others were all fairly drunk, it took a moment for
the meaning of what he had said to sink in. Then Jack's eyes
widened in shock. "Jesus!" he burst out. "I know this ya-
hoo. It's that Conrad asshole that the Colonel's been after for
so long."

Jack was standing quite close to Long Rider. So far Long
Rider had made no overtly hostile moves, had just stood there,
hands at his sides, which had lulled Jack into a false sense of
security.

But now Long Rider did move, his right hand sliding up
beneath the left lapel of his coat. It was not a hurried move,
which further confused Jack. It was a little as if the man
standing before him were about to scratch himself. But by
the time Jack began to suspect that he might be in real trouble, Long Rider's fingers were already curling around the
cool bone handle of the knife that he wore in the special
sheath sewed to his shoulder holster.

Crouching, Jack clawed for his revolver. But he was too
late. The knife flashed in the firelight, then the blade disappeared into Jack's belly, down low. Jack grunted in pain, his
fingers frozen on the butt of his pistol.

Then Long Rider twisted the blade and ripped upward,

splitting Jack open from below his navel clear to his rib cage. Jack uttered a terrible shriek as he felt his guts begin to spill out of his body.

Since Long Rider had moved so smoothly, the others were not quite sure what had happened; they were standing behind Jack and had missed the whole thing. By the time they were aware that something was terribly wrong, Jack was slowly falling forward, still screaming, his pistol forgotten as he vainly tried to hold in his guts. "Goddamn!" Pete yelled, turning around to reach for his rifle, as did the other four would-be Indian hunters.

But when they'd armed themselves and turned back toward their target, they saw with amazement that the stranger had vanished. Just melted away into the night.

A man known as Flapjack ran up to Jack, who was writhing on the ground, howling like an injured dog. "Lemme have a look," he said, trying to straighten Jack out so he could see where all the blood was coming from. But Jack only howled louder, and tried to double up again.

But Flapjack had seen enough. "Gawd," he snarled. "The bastard gutted jack like a hung hawg. I'm gonna blow his fuckin' brains out."

Flapjack took command. "He musta gone back into the brush. Pete . . . you head around to the right. There ain't much brush around the camp. We'll surround the fucker and give him some of his own medicine. We'll cut his Goddamn balls off and stuff 'em up his ass."

The men spread out, melting away into the darkness. Which was a big mistake, because they were now fighting on their adversary's terms. Flapjack discovered this when he felt an arm snake out of the darkness and circle around his neck from behind. An instant later a terrible pain made him cry out as the same knife that had gutted Jack sank into his right kidney. The agony of it was intolerable. Flapjack was trying to arch away from the pain when the knife left his kidney, rose higher, and cut his throat.

The four survivors had no trouble hearing his dying gurgles. "Jesus!" Pete shouted. "I think he got Flapjack, too."

Suddenly, going anywhere near the brush seemed like a very poor idea. The men began to drift back toward the fire. One didn't make it. He suddenly noticed that a big rock beside his path wasn't a rock at all, but by then it was too late. Even as he was trying to bring his big buffalo rifle to bear, flame lanced from the dark shapeless bulk, and a .44 caliber pistol bullet took a chunk out of his heart.

The crash of the shot actually soothed the three surviving killers. Like most white men, they had an inbred fear and loathing of knives. Gunfire they could understand, and they instinctively opened fire on the place from which the shot had come, blazing away rapidly.

No shots came back at them. They ceased firing, listening for moans that might tell them that their aim had been good. Nothing. They could hear only Jack's weakening moans, coming from behind them.

"Think we got him?" one of the men asked guardedly.

"I dunno," Pete replied. "But I think we oughta get the hell outta here."

The three of them moved instinctively closer to the apparent safety of the fire. Which proved illusory. They were gathering up their gear when one of them asked, "What're we gonna do about Jack? He sure as hell ain't in no shape to ride."

Pete shrugged. "Put one through his head, I guess. He sure ain't gonna survive with his guts hangin' in the dirt."

He abruptly straightened up. "Hey! I think I hear a horse!"

"Think the son of a bitch is runnin' off?" another man asked hopefully.

"Maybe so. I—Hell no! He's comin' this way!"

A moment later a horse and rider burst out of the darkness into the firelight. With the men already spooked by the way this stranger had been picking them off, he and his horse looked huge against the blackness behind, and the frightened men were slow in bringing up their weapons. Before they could fire more than two or three poorly aimed shots, rapid rifle fire from the horse's rider had dropped two of them.

Pete was the only survivor. Terrified, he threw away his rifle and leaped up onto the back of his unsaddled horse. A bullet cracked past his head as he pounded his heels against the horse's ribs, jolting the already frightened animal into a wild run. The horse took off so quickly that Pete was nearly thrown off backwards, but he hung on, and a moment later was racing away from the fire, over the dark plain.

Oh God! That son of a bitch was after him. He could hear the hoofbeats behind, closer and closer. The bastard was catching up!

Pursued and pursuer raced away together over the plain. The moon was nearly full; away from the fire it gave enough light so that both men could ride flat out. Long Rider, lying low against his horse's withers, felt a wild exultation flow through him as he rode. It was like the old days, a fight out in the open, the chasing down of an enemy. Only this time it was not a Crow or a Kiowa, it was a hired white killer.

The fight around the campfire, the screams of the wounded and dying, the smell of blood, had pushed him over the edge into a wild killing mood. He raced after Pete, slowly closing the distance. As he got closer, he saw Pete turn his head back toward him, saw the white blur of his face, then lower down a bright lance of flame as Pete fired a pistol in his direction.

The shot missed. Shooting backwards from a running horse, particularly while riding bareback, was not Pete's strong point. He fired again, with the same lack of effect. By now Long Rider was closing in fast, and as he closed, his old instincts returned. Killing an enemy was fine, but counting coup was even finer. As his horse came even with Pete's horse, Long Rider reached out and tapped Pete on the back with the muzzle of his Winchester.

Pete screamed, thinking for a moment that he'd been hit by a bullet. Finding that he was still in one piece, he fired his pistol again. The bullet whipped past Long Rider's face, tugging at his hair. Laughing, he struck Pete with the rifle barrel again, this time on the back of the head.

Pete slumped forward, partially stunned. But when Long Rider saw that Pete still held the pistol in his hand he finally decided that he had counted enough coup. Placing the muzzle of the rifle against Pete's side, he shot him through the body.

Pete screamed and threw up his arms. The pistol flew away into the night. Pete was slowly falling from his horse when Long Rider shot him through the head, killing him instantly.

Long Rider pulled up his horse. Six men down, none to go. Nevertheless, he rode back toward the campsite to check. As he approached, he rode cautiously; a dying man's bullet killed as surely as any other bullet.

Still out in the darkness, he dismounted and walked in on foot, checking each body. All dead, except for Jack, who was still curled up in his fetal ball, still whimpering.

Long Rider walked closer. Jack had either heard or saw him; he looked up. Agony had twisted his features into a nearly unrecognizable mask. His eyes pleaded with Long Rider.

"I should let you die slowly," Long Rider said. "Because of what you were planning to do. The innocent people you were ready to kill."

"N-no," Jack murmured.

"Go to hell then, where you belong," Long Rider replied, shooting Jack twice in the chest. Jack flopped back, finally straightening out, the horrible mess of his lower belly clearly visible. He continued to look back up at Long Rider for another moment, then died.

Long Rider remained standing over the body. As he had fired, some of the exhilaration he'd felt when he'd run down Pete had still been with him. Now he felt it leak away. There was no honor in killing men like this; it was more like stepping on cockroaches. He felt a little sickened.

He knew the source of that sickness, the source of most of the killing and suffering that had been plaguing this land.

"Harrison," he murmured. "You're a dead man."

CHAPTER TWENTY-TWO

Colonel Harlan Harrison was pacing the floor of his ranch house, back and forth, back and forth, his face screwed up into an habitual scowl. He was not used to having events go against him, and for the past few weeks they had definitely been going against him. Ever since the stranger had come to town, the mystery man, Gabe Conrad, he'd lost men, he'd lost cattle, and worst of all, he'd lost face. If he continued to lose face people would stop fearing and respecting him. And since he knew that most people hated him, without that fear, he'd be finished.

His present worry concerned the men he'd sent out toward the reservation to teach the savages a lesson. They'd been gone ten days, and still no word. He'd expected them to spend a few days roaming the reservation, picking off stray Indians, maybe even firing into the village itself. A simple enough job. They should have been back days ago. Where the hell were they? If they'd double-crossed him, if they'd taken his money and run, he'd find them if it took the rest of his life. But he'd been canny and suspicious enough to pay them only part of their blood money in advance. They would have come back to the ranch for the remainder.

He'd had men out looking for them for two days now, and still nothing. If no news came soon, he'd have to accept . . . accept what? That they'd run? That they'd . . . failed? Ridiculous. How could they fail against practically unarmed savages?

He heard a commotion out in the ranch yard. Going to a window he looked out and saw two men sliding down from lathered horses. Damn it! He didn't pay his hands to wear out his stock!

Then he noticed that the riders were two of the men he'd sent out to search for his war party. He was already walking rapidly toward the front door when the knock came. He wrenched open the door and stood glowering at the two dusty, tired men. There was no attempt to invite them in; he never let hired hands come into the house. "Well . . . what the hell did you find out?" he snapped.

The men looked nervous. "Bad news, Colonel," one said. "We found Jack and some of the others. Pete's still missin'."

Harrison knew the answer before he asked, but he asked anyhow. "Well . . . where the hell are they?"

The man gulped, then answered, "Dead, Colonel. Every man jack of 'em. We figure Pete probably got it too."

Harrison's face turned purple, and he began swearing sulfuriously. "Those Goddamned Injuns!" he screamed. "We'll take this to the army! We'll get a campaign mounted, we'll wipe out every mother's son of those fuckin' . . . ."

"We don't figure it was Injuns that done it, Colonel," the man cut in.

Harrison stopped abruptly. "No?"

"Uh-uh. We found this."

He handed Harrison a wrinkled sheet of paper containing a few lines of writing. As he positioned the paper for reading, Harrison felt cold fingers of premonition crawl up his spine. He was right. The message read: "Harrison. You're next."

It was signed, simply, "Conrad." Harrison continued to stare at the paper. He became aware that his hand was shaking. He didn't know if it was from rage or fear, but he couldn't let the men see. He whipped the paper downward, then shouted, "Tell Rex to round me up some good men. We're ridin' into town."

Half an hour later Harrison was ready to ride. He came storming out of the ranch house, dressed in his usual semi-elegance. Rex was waiting with half a dozen other men. Harrison scowled. "Not much of an escort, Rex."

Since his top gun, Dunn, had been killed—once again, by the hand of that bastard, Conrad—Rex had been responsible for ranch security and for any dirty work that needed doing. He was a barrel-chested man of medium height, maybe a little brighter than Dunn, but not quite as deadly with a gun. He looked steadily back at Harrison. "We've been losing a hell of a lot of men, Colonel. This is the most I could scrape together. But there's more in town."

Damn! Conrad was bleeding him dry of men. Literally bleeding men away. "Then hire some more," he snapped brusquely.

Rex nodded. "They won't be the best. Word's gettin' around that the Rockin' H is a dangerous outfit to work for."

"Just . . . hire some men."

During the two hour ride into town, Harrison thought hard. By the time they arrived, he had come to some conclusions. He rode straight to the Indian agent's office, finding Peebles still at his desk. As Harrison stormed into the office, he thought he detected a spasm of nervousness cross Peebles's face.

"More trouble," Harrison snapped, without even saying hello. "That madman, Conrad, killed six more of my men. Left me a note sayin' I'd be next."

Unconcealed fear twisted Peebles's features. "He . . . said the same thing about me. Left word at the reservation that he'd be coming for me."

Instead of answering, Harrison leaned his weight against the door frame and studied Peebles. He noticed a partly-filled glass of whiskey on the desk top, and even from where he stood he could smell the reek of strong spirits on Peebles's breath. He'd always known that Peebles was a weak reed, a lush, a man with little backbone. But he'd needed him. Indeed, it had been Peebles's very weakness and lack of character that had allowed Harrison to dominate him, to push him into looting the annuity payments.

But now he was beginning to wonder if those very weaknesses might be working against him. "I've been thinking, Peebles," he said softly. "Thinking that every time I tell you something, the word somehow gets around to this man, Conrad."

Peebles paled, and he half-stood. "Surely you can't think . . . ."

Harrison continued as if Peebles had not spoken. "First there was the cattle shipment. Now . . . several people knew about that, the details could have leaked out from more than one source. But the men I sent out to the reservation . . . . No one knew about that but you and me, Peebles. I didn't even tell the men what they would be doing until it was time for them to leave. So, I have a question for you, Peebles. Have you been shooting your mouth off? Maybe when you're drunk? Have you been sharing our secrets with somebody else? Maybe even working for that man Conrad?"

Peebles was about to make a hot denial, then he remembered—he'd told Rory about Harrison sending the men out to kill Indians. My God! Could Rory have . . . ?

As usual, Peebles's face gave everything away, dissolving into confusion and fear.

"You son of a bitch," Harrison snarled. "You've been sellin' me out."

"No . . . no! It's not like that at all!" Peebles protested.

Harrison came away from the door and leaned his weight on the edge of the desk. His face was now only inches away from Peebles's. Peebles shrank back into his chair, his face white. "Then just what is it like, Peebles?" Harrison asked, his voice deadly. "What is it like to sell out your partner? Did you do it for money? Did somebody pay you off? Or did you figure that if you wrecked me, you'd get to keep more for yourself?''

Peebles shook his head weakly. "No . . . it was . . . different."

A look of unutterable loathing came over Harrison's face. "You're a dead man, Peebles. You're finished. You won't have to worry about Conrad any more—if you ever did have to worry about him, if you weren't working for him all along. You'll have to worry about me. Because I'm not going to leave enough of you to even bury. But first, I'm going to make sure you pay back every damn dime you've stolen from me, even if I have to take it out of your hide."

Desperate for courage, Peebles picked up his glass and drained the rest of the whiskey. The alcohol hit almost immediately, soothing him a little, but it also added confusion to his already confused thoughts. He thought of Rory. If Rory were here now, Rory would help him. Then it occurred to him that Rory may already have helped him . . . by suggesting that he write that letter.

The thought of the letter was suddenly comforting to Peebles. Rory had warned him that Harrison would turn against him some day, and now he had. Peebles had always hated Harrison, hated the way he bullied him, made fun of him, used him. But he'd always been too afraid of Harrison to do anything about it. Harrison had all those men, all those killers on his payroll, and was never slow to use them. Peebles remembered one of the early actions, when Harrison had ordered his men to kill the Miller woman's husband. That was the first time Peebles had gotten really scared, and now it looked like Harrison was getting ready to use his killers against him, John Peebles. Just like Rory had said.

But now Peebles realized that he had the letter, or Rory had it, or maybe that big important lawyer back East already had it. Oh, God, he hoped that was true, because, as Rory had said, the letter was his only insurance against Harrison.

To Harrison's surprise, Peebles's look of fear was suddenly replaced by a look of hatred. "Your days of pushing me around are over, Harrison," he snarled. "Because if I go down, you go down too."

Harrison's eyes narrowed. "What the hell are you talkin' about?"

Peebles told him then, about the letter, about the big Eastern lawyer, about his friend, Rory Cavanaugh. The more Peebles talked, the more confident he grew, until, as he finished, his face bore a broad smirk.

But Harrison's reaction was not what he had expected. "Why . . . you stupid little shit," Harrison replied softly, almost as if he felt sorry for him. "I knew you were dumb, but this dumb?"

Peebles abruptly felt his confidence ooze away. "What do you mean?"

"I mean, you idiot, that you've been used. I've heard about this man, Cavanaugh. I've been hearing about him ever since he got to town, about the way he sits and plays poker day after day, and the way he has of asking too many clever questions. Right from the first I suspected that there was something fishy about him, and now I know what it is."

"Uh . . . what?" Peebles muttered.

Harrison slammed his fist down on the desk top. "Don't you see?" he shouted. "He's used you! Used you to get hold of everything you know about our operation. And Jesus, you even gave it to him in writing! I'll bet he's actually working for Conrad!"

Peebles slowly shook his head. He felt numb, as if a rug had been jerked out from beneath him, and he'd fallen and hit his head. No. It couldn't be true. Rory wouldn't have done that. Harrison was trying to confuse him, trying to keep him from using the letter and thus getting free.

"You're wrong," he half-whispered. "I'll prove it to you."

He got up from his desk and began to walk toward the door. "I'm going to go get Rory. He'll tell you why we did it. He'll tell you that we're friends, real friends. Then you'll see why you can't push me around any more."

As he watched Peebles walking toward the door, Harrison's

mind was working with a wild, uncontrolled speed. That damned letter! If Peebles had really been dumb enough to give it to Cavanaugh, and if Cavanaugh had sent it on to Boston, then it was all up for him. Peebles had known too much. The corrupt Republicans currently in power were his allies. The Administration's political enemies would use Peebles's letter to embarrass them. And if that happened, Harrison's supporters in Washington would drop him like a hot potato. They'd immediately throw him to the dogs, to show that they'd had no part in any of it.

Finished! As Peebles reached the door, Harrison felt an overpowering rage come over him. This gutless little bastard had finished him!

Peebles already had the door open and was stepping out onto the boardwalk when Harrison drew a pistol from beneath his coat and shot him in the back. The air whooshed out of Peebles's punctured lungs, and, throwing up his hands, he fell facedown onto the splintered wood.

Harrison walked out onto the boardwalk, recocking his pistol. Everything seemed to be happening in slow motion. He watched Peebles slowly roll over onto his back, saw the deathly pallor of his face, the disbelief in his shocked eyes.

Harrison shot him twice more, noticing the way Peebles's body jerked under the impact of each bullet. Usually Harrison paid others to do his killing. He began to realize how much enjoyment he'd been missing.

When he was sure that Peebles was dead, he shoved his pistol back into its holster. People were craning their necks out of doorways and windows. The whole damned town must have seen him shoot Peebles. Well, what the hell did it matter? He owned this town, and if anybody opened their mouths . . . .

But why worry about that? He had much bigger troubles. The letter. He had to get his hands on that letter.

Hearing the shots, some of his men had come running. Rex looked down at Peebles's dead body. He seemed very surprised, as if Harrison had shown him a side he'd never suspected was there. "You through gawking?" Harrison asked acidly.

When Rex looked up, Harrison could not tell if he were smiling or sneering. "Just admirin' your shootin', Boss."

Harrison glared at Rex. Rex looked back at him with perfect composure. He was going to have to get rid of this one, too; he'd never really trusted him.

But first, he had something for Rex to do. "Get all the boys together," Harrison snapped. "We got us a call to make."

CHAPTER TWENTY-THREE

No matter how involved he might become in a card game, Rory always sat where he could keep an eye on the door, so he was aware the moment Harrison and his men came into the saloon.

He felt an immediate sense of alarm, but hesitated; they might simply be coming in for a drink. By the time he realized they were heading straight toward him, and only for him, it was too late to do much except try to brazen it out.

He'd heard the shot that killed Peebles, the whole town had heard it, but he had no way of knowing what had happened. He smiled as Harrison came to a stop about six feet away, and stood glaring down at him. "Hello, Colonel," he said affably. "Care to play?"

"The charade's over, Cavanaugh," Harrison replied icily. "No more games."

"Why, Colonel . . . whatever are you talking about?" Damned if he'd eat shit in front of this empty bag of wind.

"The letter, Cavanaugh. I want it."

Rory stopped smiling. "You'll have to be more specific, Harrison. What letter?"

"The letter you had Peebles write. A letter full of lies about me."

Now the significance of that single gunshot began to sink into Rory, and he realized that this encounter might be even more serious than he had thought. Obviously Harrison had a pretty good idea of what he had been doing. Rory began to regret that he had not immediately gone for his gun the moment Harrison and his men came through the doorway. Well . . . maybe not. There were eight of them, not counting Harrison, all of them hard-looking men. He doubted that his little .32 would have done him much good against so much firepower. Better to see if he could bargain his way out of this one. "Were they lies?" he asked the colonel.

A spasm of anger passed across Harrison's face. Then he turned and nodded to Rex. "Have the men bring him along to my hotel room."

The men moved in around Rory. He did not resist when they jerked him to his feet, not even when they removed his Smith and Wesson from its shoulder holster. Harrison was already heading toward the doorway. The man he'd called Rex prodded Rory along, with the rest of the men following. Rory wondered if he should make a break for it when he reached the door; they were not guarding him too closely. Maybe he could grab hold of Harrison, take Harrison's gun, and hold him as a hostage.

Uh-uh. As soon as he reached the doorway Rex and the others fanned out around him, and kept prodding him along toward the hotel. Rory noticed a crowd gathered further up the street, near Peebles's office. Harrison saw where he was looking. "Your 'friend'," he said with a sneer. "I think he found the price of betrayal a little high."

Rory felt a cold shiver run up his spine. This was getting more and more serious. If Harrison had killed Peebles so openly, what were his own chances of survival?

And then he saw something that gave him hope. Someone, actually; Kate was standing about forty yards away, looking straight at him. He suddenly stopped walking. "Damned if

I'm going to your room, Harrison,'' he snapped. ''You're not my type.''

The men closed in around him more tightly. Harrison jerked his head angrily at Rex, who produced a pistol and placed it against Rory's head. Rory heard the hammer click back. ''Do like the boss says,'' Rex snarled. ''Or I'll splatter your brains all over town.''

Rory nodded docilely, then began walking toward the hotel again. He'd gotten what he wanted. He was sure that Kate had seen the whole thing, would know that he had been found out and captured. And if she knew, Gabe would soon know.

Which wouldn't do him much good for the time being. He was hustled into Harrison's hotel room, and pushed up against the wall. He noticed that it was a much larger and fancier room than his own.

Harrison moved directly in front of him. ''I want that letter.''

Rory shrugged. He was not about to deny that the letter existed; its existence was his main chance of surviving the next few hours. ''I don't have it,'' he said.

''Then who does?''

''A lawyer in Boston.''

Rory saw Harrison's face blanch; his worst fears had been realized. ''I want his name,'' Harrison said, his voice tight.

Rory laughed. ''He's far too important a man for you to buffalo, Harrison. Forget it, it's too late for that kind of thing.''

Harrison's face grew livid. ''I'll decide that!'' he screamed. ''His name! I want his name!''

Rory was unprepared for the sudden blow Harrison slammed into his face. He reeled backwards against the wall. His first reaction was rage; he wanted to hit Harrison back, but Rex stepped in close, pointing his pistol at Rory's chest.

The blow was not repeated. Harrison stood back a few paces, a pained look on his face as he nursed his bruised knuckles. ''Are you going to give me his name?'' he asked again.

Rory shook his head. By now it was pretty clear that Harrison was coming unglued. In his present condition it was impossible to forecast with any certainty what he might do. It was even possible that he might send some kind of message to confederates back East and order Rory's grandfather killed.

"Even if I gave you the name, it wouldn't help," Rory said calmly. "By now he's passed the information along. There are too many people who already know."

He was not positive that was true, but he was not about to admit it to Harrison. But Harrison guessed anyhow. "As I said, I'll be the judge of that," he replied, smiling a ghastly smile. "I'll warn you once more . . . if you don't tell me immediately, Rex and the boys will beat it out of you."

Rory forced a smile; it was important that he not show fear, although he was getting pretty damned nervous. "You try roughing me up," he threatened, "and I'll make the most god-awful bunch of noise you ever heard."

Harrison hesitated. A little while ago he'd gunned down John Peebles in cold blood. No, in hot blood. In front of witnesses. That was before he had thought out the full implications of this letter thing. Now he realized that his tail was caught in a mighty tight crack.

But there might be ways to extricate himself. He could claim that the letter was a fake, that he'd caught Peebles cheating the Indians, and that Peebles had tried to blackmail him with the letter. He could claim that he'd killed Peebles in self-defense, after Peebles had tried to silence him. Sure, people had seen him shoot Peebles in the back. But there were ways to make witnesses forget, ways to put a different interpretation on what they'd seen. Yes . . . there might still be a possibility of surviving this disaster.

But not if he noisily tortured Cavanaugh in plain daylight in his hotel room. Everyone had seen him bring Cavanaugh in here, some of the nosier among the town's citizens were probably outside listening right now.

He abruptly turned toward Rex. "We'll keep him here for

an hour or so. Then some of the boys can take him on out to
the ranch. All nice and friendly-like.''

He turned toward Rory and grinned. ''You'll like the ranch.
Out there, you can scream all you want.''

After she had watched Harrison and his men take Rory
away, Kate got into her buggy and rode straight out of town.
She knew Harrison, she knew that Rory would have to get
help soon, or he'd be a dead man. Like her husband. A spasm
of hatred shot through her as she thought of Harrison, of the
things he'd done to her and to hers. Now her only hope,
Rory's only hope, was Gabe.

She had left Gabe about five miles out of town. He'd come
to the ranch the night before. They'd talked, and had deter-
mined that it was time for the final showdown with Harrison.
Peebles's letter had been sent long enough ago; it must now
be in the right hands. With such a big scandal in the offing,
people in high places would do little to help Harrison.

It had been a wonderful night for Kate. Not only did it
look like the end for her enemy, but Gabe had made love to
her, wonderful love. When they set out for town in the morning, Kate had felt warm inside, both from sexual satiation
and from the prospect of complete revenge on Harrison.

The plan had been for Gabe to stay near town while Kate
went in to fetch Rory. Then Gabe and Rory would ride together to take care of Peebles and Harrison. But then Kate
had seen Rory being taken away by Harrison and his men.

And . . . Peebles. Kate had been shocked by the sight of
Peebles's dead body lying right out there in the open, a government official murdered in broad daylight. Harrison must
be losing his mind. Which made Rory's danger all the greater.

She ran the buggy into the little copse in which Gabe had
concealed himself. As he left cover and walked out to join
her, he sensed that there was trouble. ''Where's Rory?'' he
asked.

''Harrison has him.''

She told what she had seen, about Rory, and about Peebles,

too. He questioned her as to how many men Harrison had with him, how closely they were guarding Rory. "I have to go in and get him," Gabe said.

"No. You may not have to. I . . . took a chance. I know you told me not too, but I figured, with Rory taken, things had changed. So I listened outside Harrison's hotel window. Like Rory told us, it's right by the alley, and Harrison had the drapes drawn, so he couldn't see me. I heard him order his men to take Rory out to the ranch in about an hour. They should be on their way now. Did I do all right?"

For the first time since she'd told him about Rory, Gabe smiled. "Yes. Fantastic. Now . . . it'd probably be best if you go back to town, where you can keep an eye on things. If Harrison doesn't ride out with Rory and the others, it'll be important to know where he is, what he's doing."

"Of course. But . . . where will you be?"

Now his smile grew colder. "Collecting Rory."

There were only four men guarding Rory. But all four were armed, and he was not, and Harrison had ordered the men to kill him instantly if he made a break for it. As they escorted him out of town, they rode around him in a diamond pattern, with a man on either side, one ahead, and one behind.

He went along meekly, hoping to lull them by his passivity. He knew he'd have to make a break for it sooner or later; if they got him all the way to the ranch he was as good as dead.

They were about four miles out of town when he spotted Gabe's ambush. Gabe had left the usual sign for him, one they'd decided on a couple of years before, during another tight squeeze . . . a peculiarly shaped mark carved into the bark of a tree.

And there it was, about a hundred yards ahead, the escape route, a trail leading off the main trail into high, thick brush.

His guards had grown progressively more lax. And why not? The man on Rory's right had hold of the reins of his horse. If Rory tried to snatch them back and make a run for it, they'd have him before he'd gone ten yards.

The man to his rear had ridden further up on Rory's left, to talk to the man guarding that potential avenue of escape. He was a real joker; all four guards were listening to what he had to say, laughing at his stories, some of which concerned the fun Rory was going to have once the boss had him alone on his own ground.

They were still laughing as they came abreast of that little trail. Rory glanced down it. The trail branched off to the right, disappearing into ten-foot high scrub. His captors were still laughing when the thunderous roar of a Sharps rifle, fired at close range, blasted them all into silence.

The man on Rory's right was literally picked up out of his saddle by the Sharps's huge bullet. He was still in the air when Rory, his reins now free, jerked his horse to the right and raced away down the little trail.

He heard shouting behind; at least one of the men was after him. Then he saw it a few yards ahead, a Winchester rifle lying on a rock alongside the trail. Rory scooped up the rifle, then turning, aimed it at the man pounding along after him. He had a moment to see the surprise in the man's eyes, then Rory shot him out of the saddle.

Rory heard the Sharps roar again. He raced past the fallen guard, back toward the main trail. As he came out into the open he saw Gabe riding out of the brush, the smoking Sharps held in one hand, muzzle pointing skyward. "I was going to ride after you . . . make sure you were all right," Gabe said.

Rory grinned. God, it felt good to be alive, to have a rifle in his hands again, to be free of whatever fate Harrison had had in store for him. "I killed the other one," he said.

He was looking around for bodies. He saw only two. "The fourth one got away," Gabe said regretfully. "Rode away like a pack of wild hogs was after him."

Rory stopped grinning. "He'll warn Harrison."

Gabe nodded. "I don't mind. I like the idea of Harrison sitting in town, sweating."

"We're going after him, then."

The look in Gabe's eyes chilled Rory. "Yes," Gabe replied in a low, controlled voice. "Harrison is a dead man."

Rory nodded, remembering Harrison's fist smashing into his face. "He is indeed."

Once back in town, Kate did her best to keep out of sight while at the same time keeping tabs on Harrison. She was standing half-hidden behind her buggy when she saw a man come racing into town on a well-lathered horse. She recognized him as one of the men who'd been guarding Rory.

The man was obviously scared; he made no attempt at quiet or concealment. "Colonel," he bellowed as he slid down from his horse in front of the hotel. "We were bushwhacked. Cavanaugh got away."

Harrison immediately came out onto the boardwalk. His face was white as he listened to the man's report. This was bad. If he'd been able to make Cavanaugh convincingly 'disappear' he might have been able to put this whole damn mess behind him. But with Cavanaugh alive and talking . . . .

But now, new hope. "I think they're on their way into town," the gunhand was telling him. "I looked back a couple of times, saw two men ridin' after me, about a mile or so behind."

Oh God, Harrison thought desperately. If they'd only be that stupid. If they came into town he'd have them. Cavanaugh and Conrad too, because he had little doubt that the other man was Conrad.

He immediately began giving orders. "Rex . . . get the boys together. Tell me how many we got."

Kate, still behind her buggy about forty yards away, watched while Harrison paced back and forth along the boardwalk. Rex returned about five minutes later, and even from where she stood, partially hidden, she could see that he did not look happy. "Only six, Colonel. 'Sides you an' me."

"Six?" Harrison asked incredulously. "There are certainly more than that!"

Rex shook his head. "Nope. About a dozen more lit out. They were kinda shook up by that thing with Peebles. And maybe a little tired o' seein' their friends get killed by Conrad, an' maybe thinkin' they'll be next. I been kinda wonderin' the same thing myself."

Rex was looking speculatively at Harrison. Harrison, apparently thunderstruck by his sudden reversal of fortunes, gasped a few times, then his face hardened. "Rex," he said softly. "If you stand by me, if you get the other six to stand by me too . . . then I'll see that you get five thousand dollars cash."

Rex smiled. "Now . . . that just might make it worth my while."

Kate watched while Rex positioned his six men around the town, four of them guarding the main street, two more posted on the roof of the hotel, the town's highest building. Harrison and Rex remained near the center, partly because Harrison was not about to be left on his own. Not with a man like Gabe Conrad heading his way.

Kate was in a frenzy, not sure what to do. So far either Harrison had not seen her, or, seeing her, had not, under the weight of his current problems, considered her worth worrying about. That might be a help. She was going to have to do something. She wasn't about to let her, well, her lover get shot down by Harrison and his gang. That bastard was not going to take another man away from her!

She took her shotgun from beneath the buggy's seat, then slipped quietly away into an alley. The shotgun was very big, and not easy to carry, a ten-gauge, double-barreled monster, loaded with buckshot. Her husband had gotten her to fire it a couple of times, but she was terrified of its massive recoil.

Her plan was simple. When Gabe and Rory started into town, she'd try and shoot the men on the hotel roof. Even if she missed, her men would have some warning of the trap set for them. Even if cost her own life.

The waiting was a terrible strain. She had hidden herself behind some large barrels. She was very uncomfortable. The

afternoon drew on. It had been late in the day when the es-
caping gunhand had ridden into town. Evening would fall
soon; the light was already starting to go. Where were Gabe
and Rory?

Kate's nerves were by now so tightly strung that she almost
screamed when she felt a hand settle onto her shoulder. She
spun, trying to bring the shotgun barrel around before they
killed her . . . only to find herself staring, openmouthed, at
Gabe.

"My . . . my God!" she hissed. "Where did you come
from?"

"Shhhhh. We knew they had to be waiting. I came in from
the side, up that little dry creek bed. Rory's waiting with the
horses up near the woods. Are you all right?"

He had noticed the shotgun, and he was touched. This was
one brave woman, maybe as brave as a Lakota girl, which
was good, because it was time to fight. "Do you know where
they are?" he asked.

She nodded. "Four in the street, facing where the trail
comes out of the woods. Two more on the hotel roof.
Harrison's with one man down by the saloon."

Gabe looked up at the hotel roof. "Thanks," he said, and
began to slip away up the alley.

"Thanks? Is that all?" she muttered. But Gabe was already
too far away to hear. She watched, awed by the silent way he
moved, the way he seemed to just float along from one patch
of cover to the next. A moment later he was gone from sight.

Kate now forgotten, all his senses honed for battle, Gabe
slipped along one side of the hotel. Going around to the back,
he climbed noiselessly up onto the high porch that protected
the kitchen entrance. From there it was easy to use a window
frame to hitch himself up onto the roof itself.

There they were, as Kate had said, two men, crouched
behind the low parapet that overlooked the main street, rifles
ready. Gabe had the Sharps hanging across his back from a
sling. He now worked the rifle free carefully, then lay it quietly beside him. He would not need it yet.

There was a lot of good cover on the roof, several skylights, for the hotel had pretensions. It took Gabe five minutes to work his way past two of the skylights, until he was less than six feet from one of the riflemen. Each rifleman was screened from the other by another skylight, they could not see one another. Nor would they ever see one another again.

Gabe drew his knife, slipped around the skylight. His target was busy staring up the street, he was not even aware anyone was behind him until Gabe's left hand grabbed his face from behind, covering his mouth, while the knife slashed deep into his throat.

But the other rifleman heard the brief scuffle, perhaps even the wheezing sigh as his companion's final breath hissed from the gaping, blood-spraying wound in his throat. "Hank? What the hell are you doin' over there?"

There was no answer. "Hank?" the man whispered anxiously. "You there?"

Again no answer. Now the man was really alarmed. "Goddamn it, Hank . . . you ain't run out on me, have you?"

He slithered across the roof top toward his partner's position. As he rounded the edge of the skylight he was relieved to see Hank still lying in place . . . until he saw the blood, oceans of blood.

And then a dark figure was hurtling toward him. He tried to ward off his attacker, but a hand grabbed him by the throat and he felt a terrible searing pain as a long-bladed knife lanced up under his ribcage into his heart. He had one moment to stare, terror-stricken, into a pair of cold gray eyes, and then he was forever finished with seeing.

Gabe let the body fall, then carefully wiped his knife clean on his latest victims' clothing, before putting it back into its underarm sheath.

Now the roof was his. He retrieved his Sharps and took up a position behind the parapet, where one of the rifleman had been stationed earlier. He could see all the way up the street. It was completely deserted. The town's population, aware of an impending gunfight, had hidden itself behind walls and doors.

But Gabe thought he saw movement further up the street. Yes . . . there . . . a man hidden behind a watering trough. Gabe could see the barrel of his rifle. Then he saw another man, crouched in a doorway. There should be two more somewhere.

But time was running out. The light looked about right, Rory should be making his move soon. Yes, here it came. Along with the other waiting men Gabe could hear the distant sound of hoofbeats. Back in the woods, someone was running a horse, hard, toward the town.

A moment later the horse burst out of the woods and started down the main street. Waiting, hidden men tensed themselves. Then it became obvious that the horse was riderless, that it was a trick to make the defenders show themselves.

The men Gabe had already spotted pulled back into their cover, but too late. Gabe's Sharps roared, and the man in the doorway was slammed back against the building. The man behind the watering trough automatically ducked low, but he was expecting trouble to come from up the street, not from behind, so Gabe's next shot was an easy one. Four down so far.

By now, all was confusion. "One of 'em's up on top of the hotel!" Gabe heard a man cry out. There was so much confusion that at first nobody noticed a second horse racing into town from the direction of the woods. But this horse was not riderless, Rory was up on its back, Winchester ready, and as the two men still guarding that end of town faced toward the hotel, he was able to open up on them.

One went down immediately, shot through the head. The other, yelping with fright, turned to fight, levering his Winchester as he fired at Rory, but Rory was coming on fast, swerving his horse from side to side, firing back.

Alarmed, the gunman started to turn, to run, but it was too late. Rory shot him down, sending three bullets into his body.

Gabe had already left the hotel roof, slipping through a

trapdoor into the main upstairs hallway. He pounded down the stairs, heading for the front door. If Kate was right, there should be only two men left. Harrison and one of his hired guns.

Rex had been hunkered down behind a water barrel. He saw Gabe the moment he stepped out onto the boardwalk. Rex was no idiot, he wasn't about to give his life for Harrison, but there was that five thousand dollars to think about. A man could do a lot with five thousand dollars, live well for years. To earn that money there were only two men to take care of. Kill this one, and the other would be easy.

Gabe spotted Rex a moment after Rex spotted him. It was almost too late. Rex had his Winchester against his shoulder, aiming it. Gabe immediately rolled to his right; no time to use the Sharps. As he rolled, he clawed for his right-hand .44. A bullet smacked into the wall directly behind where he'd been standing.

Rex was frantically changing his aim as Gabe came up onto one knee, his right hand full of .44. But the speed of Gabe's maneuver had unnerved Rex; he'd been sure he had the bastard, and then he suddenly wasn't where he was supposed to be.

Rex's next shot missed, but Gabe's didn't. The bullet took Rex just below the ribs, not a killing shot, but one that slammed Rex backwards. Fighting for breath, he tried to lever another round into the chamber of his rifle, but he knew he wasn't going to make it; Gabe was on his feet now, coming toward him, firing. Two more bullets hit Rex, both in the chest, and as he fell he said a final goodbye to the five thousand dollars.

Gabe was now in the middle of the street. He took a cautious step toward his fallen opponent, wanting to make sure he was out of the fight for good. He was totally unaware of the man who'd stepped out of another doorway directly behind him. Colonel Harlan Harrison.

Harrison had grown increasingly horrified as he saw his ambush fall apart. Now, as far as he could tell, all his men were dead. Which meant that he would probably soon be dead, too.

But he'd be damned if he'd go alone. He'd never actually met Gabe Conrad, but he'd heard descriptions, and the long hair, the height, and the leather coat with the painting of the Thunderbird across its back left little doubt that the man who'd just killed Rex was Conrad himself. A wave of hatred swept over Harrison. This was the man who had ruined him! He raised his pistol, aiming at Gabe's unprotected back. God-damn it, he'd make sure Conrad joined him in hell!

But Harrison was unaware that danger threatened him from behind, too. Galvanized by all the shooting, Kate was unable to remain hidden in the alley. Clutching her shotgun, she reached the main street just in time to see Gabe walking slowly toward a man who lay on his back in the middle of the street, and in time to see Harrison, her hated enemy, step out of a doorway and aim a pistol at her lover's back.

She was never really aware of raising the shotgun, and only vaguely aware of screaming, "Harrison! You bastard!"

The shotgun roared, its recoil slamming Kate backward; she had pulled too hard; she'd set off both barrels. Startled by her cry, Harrison had started to turn, and as he turned, the buckshot hit him in the shoulder, blowing his right arm away from his body.

He staggered backwards, not quite sure what had happened, aware only of a strange feeling in his right shoulder, not exactly a pain, just something that felt . . . wrong.

Then he looked down and saw it, the red, ragged mess where his arm had previously joined his body, and the arm itself lying a few feet away, its dead hand still clutching his pistol.

He started screaming, a high thin scream with little force to it. Horrified, agonized, he reeled across the street, blood pouring from his ghastly wound. Finally he fell, but still he kept screaming.

Gabe walked up to Harrison, and began cocking his pistol. "No!" he heard Kate shout. Then she was pushing him out of the way. He stood to one side, watching as she glared down at Harrison, then fumbled in the pocket of her dress for another shotgun shell. She dropped the shell. Gabe bent down and picked it up, handed it to her. Her eyes met his for a moment. Hot, crazy eyes.

Kaplonk. The big shell slid into the shotgun's breech. Kate slammed it shut. Harrison was aware of her now, aware that it was Kate who had blown off his arm. "You . . . you . . . ." he whimpered.

Fear churned Harrison's belly. He was horribly aware of the wildness of Kate's eyes as she sighted down those big twin barrels, aiming at his head, aware of the huge black holes at the end of those barrels. "No . . . ." he managed to say feebly, just once. Then the shotgun roared again.

Staring down at what was left of Colonel Harlan Harrison's head, Kate began to shake. She never felt the shotgun fall from her hands, but was aware of a strong arm supporting her, of a voice murmuring something into her ear. She felt somewhat comforted, but not enough. Not nearly enough.

Strange. Vengeance wasn't at all what she'd expected it to be.

CHAPTER TWENTY-FOUR

As Kate walked along the boardwalk, she didn't know whether she liked the new way people looked at her or not. Some of them were afraid of her; they'd seen what her shotgun had done to Colonel Harrison. Others seemed admiring; many had hated Harrison.

Of course, some respected her for her money. Kate was now a fairly wealthy woman. During all the confusion after Harrison's death, she had hired several men, and, riding onto Harrison's land, had removed one hell of a lot of his cattle. No one stopped her; all of Harrison's hired hands had made a run for it, and as far as anyone knew, there were no heirs.

Kate felt no guilt about expropriating all those cattle; Harrison owed her. And along with all those extra cattle, she had also picked up the government grazing leases previously owned by Harrison. She had a big spread now, she was one of the most prosperous ranchers in the territory. She knew her dead husband would have been proud of her.

Gabe had stayed on for a while. He'd seemed a little amused by the energy she expended building up her spread before anyone else could move in on Harrison's defunct empire. Once or twice she'd caught him covertly studying her, as if she were some rare creature that defied understanding. From time to time she'd wondered herself at the unexpected inner compulsion that drove her on . . . until she finally gave in and admitted that she had always wanted to be rich, to be someone of consequence.

That knowledge had softened the blow when Gabe left one day, simply left. It was a few days after the new Indian agent had arrived to fill John Peebles's vacant position. Gabe had gone into town to see him, had disappeared into the office with the man for half an hour. Everyone in town had already pegged the new agent as the usual carpetbagger out to make his fortune, but after Gabe's little talk the agent had seemed a changed man. Actually, a somewhat nervous man. The entire territory later remarked on how zealously he guarded the interests of the Indians out there on the reservation.

And then Gabe had ridden away. Just ridden away. Packed up his horse and ridden out of Kate's life. He'd said goodbye, said it gently. She hadn't begged, hadn't said anything, although she was afraid that her eyes might be begging. "I can't stay," he had said quietly. "This is not my life."

She understood. Already his eyes were drifting away toward the horizon. She thought for a moment of asking to go with him, then was surprised by the fierce rush of possessiveness that swept over her, possessiveness for her land, her cattle, her ranch, and she knew with certainty where her heart truly belonged.

So she watched him ride away, once again wearing the long linen duster and big slouch hat, just another wandering trail bum. But she knew better, knew so much better.

Kate was so lost in her recollections that she almost collided with another pedestrian. There was a moment of maneuvering, then the man she had almost run into was doffing his hat. "Why . . . good morning, Mrs. Miller."

"Good morning, Mr. Johnson."

Matt Johnson was a newcomer to the area. Obviously a man of means, he had bought land adjoining Kate's land. He was cultured, apparently honest, and . . . why not admit it . . . very handsome.

Kate tried to conceal her admiration . . . until she noticed the answering admiration in Matt's eyes. For just one moment she let her thoughts drift back to a tall quiet man with light grey eyes.

She shook her head; she felt a little dizzy. "Is something wrong, Mrs. Miller?" she heard Matt ask.

She shook her head again. "No. Nothing at all."

She smiled, aware that she had a fine smile, then offered her arm. "Perhaps, Mr. Johnson, you'd care to accompany me to the store?"